Penguin Books
Tarry Flynn

Patrick Kavanagh was born in County Monaghan
in 1904. The son of a farmer and cobbler, he grew
up surrounded by those 'stony-grey hills' where so
much of his poetry had its inspiration. He left
school apparently destined to become a small
farmer, but 'I dabbled in verse,' he said, 'and it
became my life.' At the age of thirty he left
Inniskeen to walk fifty miles to Dublin. In 1936 his
first book of verse, *Ploughman and Other Poems*,
was published, and in 1938 he followed this up with
The Green Fool, an autobiography. He spent the
lean years of the war in Dublin, when Cyril
Connolly published his long poem 'The Great
Hunger' in *Horizon*. After the war he published
this novel and two more collections of verse,
A Soul for Sale and *Come Dance with Kitty
Stobling*. The bulk of his verse was included in
his *Collected Poems*, and some of his prose in
Collected Pruse. He died in 1967 and is buried in
his native Inniskeen.

Patrick Kavanagh

Tarry Flynn

Penguin Books

Penguin Books Ltd, Harmondsworth,
Middlesex, England
Penguin Books, 625 Madison Avenue,
New York, New York 10022, U.S.A.
Penguin Books Australia Ltd, Ringwood,
Victoria, Australia
Penguin Books Canada Ltd, 2801 John Street,
Markham, Ontario, Canada L3R 1B4
Penguin Books (N.Z.) Ltd, 182–190 Wairau Road,
Auckland 10, New Zealand

First published by The Pilot Press 1948
This edition first published by Martin Brian &
O'Keeffe 1972
Published in Penguin Books 1978

Made and printed in Great Britain by
C. Nicholls & Company Ltd
Set in Monotype Times

1

'Where the devil did I put me cap? Did any of you see me cap?'
Tarry Flynn was standing on a stool searching on the top of the
dresser. He lifted an old school book that lay in the dust of the
dresser-top and temporarily suspending the search for his cap was
taking a quick glance at the tattered pages.

His mother, who had just come down stairs and was sitting in
her bare feet by the fire with her shoes beside her on the floor,
forgot for a moment the corn on her little toe which she had been
fondling and said with exasperation:

'What in the name of the devil's father are you looking for at
such an hour of the morning? Are you going to go to Mass at
all or do you mean to be home with them atself?' She swung
round. 'Looking on top of the dresser! Mind you don't put the
big awkward hooves on one of them chickens that's under you.'

Tarry glanced down at the hen and chickens that were picking
crumbs off the floor. 'A fine bloody place to have them,' he said.

'They'll make more money than you anyway,' said the mother.
'Well, of all the mane men that ever was you're the manest. Of a
holyday morning to be looking for the oul' cap at twenty-five
minutes past eight. Anything to be late for Mass. And if it wasn't
the cap it 'id be something else – the stud or there 'id be a button
off the coat. Just like your uncle Petey that never gave himself
more than five minutes to walk to Mass. I remember him and he'd
keep looking at himself and looking at himself in the looking
glass till, honest to God, it 'id make a body throw off their guts
to see him.'

'Ah don't be bothering me.'

'Oh, that's your uncle all over. Nobody could talk to him;
he knew everything. He'd take on to put a leg in a horse – and the
whole country laughing at him. Will you get down to hell out of
that and go to Mass? On the blessed day of Corpus Christi to

think of a man sling-slanging about the house and first Mass near half over.'

'Amn't I taking the bike, I tell you.'

'Hens not fed, the pot not on for the pigs – and you washed your face in the well water, about as much as we'll have what 'ill make the breakfast.'

Mrs Flynn had stuck her feet in her shoes. She rose and looked out the window. 'Where's this one?' she asked in a growl.

'I'm here,' called 'this one', who was Mary, a daughter, from upstairs.

'Lord God of Almighty, but you're another of the Sunday girls. Lying up there in bed like a churn a-drying that – that– Have you any shame at all in you?'

'Shut up,' the daughter shouted down.

'Oh, it's me has the good family that I ought to be proud of,' the mother said with broad irony. 'If it's not this man here it's one of yous. That's what left the Carlins where they are – getting up, one of them at eight and the other at nine, making two breakfasts. If they had one breakfast now they wouldn't be as hard to talk to. When you're coming down don't forget to bring down that vessel and not have a smell in the room that 'id knock a dog down. I want it to feed the calves anyhow.'

Mrs Flynn crossed the floor and stared out the back window. She had to screw her eye at the corner of the window to get a full view of the Drumnay lane where, at the top of a rise behind the house, it joined the main road. The whitethorn hedges heavy with summer leaves could give Tarry's imagination the idea of a tropical jungle, but the mother did not like those hedges.

'There, it's now half eight and no sign of you going.'

'Don't I know well you put that clock on a half hour last night,' Tarry said.

'I didn't nor half a minute.'

Mary came down the stairs carrying a bucket. Standing in the doorway for a moment she glanced up and down the road to see if anyone was coming or going. Then she dashed across the street and flung the contents of the bucket against the face of the dung-hill.

6

She returned to the house with her fist in her yawning mouth. 'A terrible close morning,' she said.

'Did you look to see if the hen in the barrel broke any of the eggs?' the mother asked her.

'None, as far as I could see.'

'I wouldn't put it past you but you didn't look at all. Will you try and get this fellow his cap and get him away to Mass – the oul' haythen!' She turned to her son, who was now sitting on the edge of the table by the front window lighting a cigarette.

'Lord! Lord! Lord!' she exclaimed, 'starting to puff at the curse-o'-God fag at such an hour of the morning. Have you any cutting-up in you at all?' Crossing the floor she looked out the front window. 'I see that young calf out there licking at the dirty hen's dishes and he'll get a scour out of it as sure as God's in Heaven.'

'There's the oul' cap,' said Mary, lifting an old newspaper that lay in the back window. 'He must be blind that he couldn't get it.'

'Didn't want to get it,' said the mother. 'Will you, like a dacent girl, run out to the cart-house and see if his bike is pumped?'

'It's hard enough,' she said when she came in again, 'it 'ill carry him.'

The mother hung on the kettle and began to turn the fan bellows wheel. With her left hand she poked the fire with a long pot-stick and her handling of that pot-stick showed better than her talk her annoyance with her son. 'A poor thing,' she growled as she stirred up the clinkers and dragged them aside, 'a poor thing to rear a man that doesn't care for God, man or the devil. And him knowing as well as the head's on his body that I have to go to the market this day with them cocks that we caught last night. I hope I'll be able to swop them for pullets,' she was now addressing her daughter. 'I won't get very big pullets for them, but they're good March chickens and I oughtn't to do too bad . . . Lord, O Lord! Aggie left here to go to Mass at five minutes to eight and there's that man still steaming away at the fag like a railway engine. Take Carroll's factory to keep him in fags. Mary,

7

go up the loft steps and see if you can see Bridie coming with the milk. We haven't a drop for the breakfast that that fellow there didn't slug into the long gut of his before he went to bed last night. Tarry, will you for my sake and for everybody's sake get up and go to Mass?'

'I'm always an hour too soon when I go by you,' said Tarry.

'I'll quit talking, I'll quit talking,' the mother sighed.

Bridie passed in front of the window carrying the cans of milk and trying to keep the calf from knocking the lids off.

'The strawberry is looking the bull,' Bridie said when she laid the cans down in the kitchen. 'She didn't give me half as much milk as she ought to.'

'She couldn't be looking the bull, I don't think,' said the mother, making a mental calculation. 'She took the bull a fortnight ago, and unless she was the devil's ranter altogether she wouldn't be coming round till three weeks. Be a terrible loss if she won't keep the bull,' she reflected pensively.

'There's a lot of cows going wrong that way,' said Bridie.

'Will you,' the mother shouted at Tarry, 'hurry up and be home early from Mass in case you have to go with that cow. We'd have to sell her a stripper if she doesn't keep the bull.'

'The white cow has a tear on her teat that's a total dread,' Bridie said, 'like a tear from a buck wire.'

'Oh, that's more of this man's doing!' cried the mother. 'How many times did I tell him to fix that paling and not have the buck wire trailing half way across the field. To look at this place a person would think we hadn't a man about it. Do you think will the teat need to be bathed? Oh, look at him there with his big nose on him and the oul' cod of a face like his uncle that – that a Protestant wouldn't be worse than him . . .'

'And there's more than that, the dirty oul' dog,' said Bridie. 'There's other things going on that might get us all into trouble.'

'Arra, what?' the mother cried, very dramatically.

Bridie was being mysterious. 'If some fellows we know are not in jail before the next week or so I'll be surprised.'

'God, O God! O God! O God!' lamented the mother. 'Is it something to do with this fella here?'

'Huh! Is that the way it's with you? A girl knocked off her bicycle at Drumnay cross and there's going to be a lot of trouble about it.'

The mother had heard enough to drive her to the heights of dramatic intensity. By the tone of her daughter's voice she knew that something really desperate must have been done to some girl.

'Was heavy hands laid on some poor girl?' she asked. Heavy hands was a term Mrs Flynn had for the worst that a man could do to a woman. 'And who was she?'

'Mary Reilly,' said Bridie. 'Whatever was done to her I don't know only what I heard.'

Tarry, finishing his cigarette, was trying his best to defeat the discussion with a sneer. But the drama was beating him.

'It's all nonsense,' he said, 'all nonsense.'

The mother started to cry. 'Isn't it a poor thing that I can't have one day's peace with the whole rick-ma-tick of yous? Amn't I the heart-broken woman? And me going to the market the day. I won't be the better of this for a week.'

'Quit whinging anyway,' said the daughter.

'How can I quit! how can I quit!' She suddenly rallied sufficiently to say to Bridie: 'Go and strain that milk into the big pan-crock before you feed the hens ... And what was done to the girl?' she asked Tarry when the daughters were absent.

'Nothing,' said Tarry, 'nothing.'

'There be to be something or Bridie wouldn't have it. Lord, O Lord! why can't you be like another and not have us the talk of the country? Not that I care a straw for that whipster of Reilly's – a big-faced stuck-up thing that ... a bit of mauling wouldn't do her much harm. But you to get your name up with it, that's what I can't stand. It's a pity you wouldn't try to keep away from that cross. Get up now and go to Mass and be back quick in case you have to go to Kerley's with that cow.'

The mother's imagination followed her son as he cycled down the lane towards the main road. She loved that son more than any mother ever loved a son. She hardly knew why. There was something so natural about him, so real and so innocent and

9

which yet looked like badness. He hated being in time for Mass. He had always slept soundly through the Rosary in the days when his father was alive to say that evening prayer. And he was forever reading and dreaming to himself in the fields. It was a risk to let him out alone in a horse and cart. The heart was often out of her mouth that he'd turn the cart upside down in a gripe while he was dreaming or looking at the flowers. And then the shocking things that he sometimes said about religion and the priests. She was very worried about all that. Not that she loved the priests – like a true mother she'd cut the Pope's throat for the sake of her son – but she felt the power of the priests and she didn't want to have their ill-will.

He was a queer son in some ways. There was a kink in him which she never had been able to fathom.

The sun shone on the little hills. Hens were flying over gates and fences to scratch in potato and turnip fields.

The headlands and the hedges were so fresh and wonderful, so gay with the dawn of the world. Tarry never tired looking at these ordinary things as he tired of the Mass and of religion. In a dim way he felt that he was not a Christian. In the god of Poetry he found a God more important to him than Christ. His god had never accepted Christ.

Then the place of things alive overflowed his analytic thoughts and he heard the robins and sparrows in the hedges. A crib cart with a load of young pigs passed on its way to the market, for as well as being a Church holyday this was also a big market day in the local town. Ahead of him at the Miskin lane he could see another late Mass-goer whose walk he recognized. A good friend of his own, a poetic man who disliked being in time for Mass as much as Tarry. This was Eusebius Cassidy, his young neighbour. Eusebius was on foot, which meant that Tarry would catch up with him.

'Hello,' Tarry said as he slowed down and cycled beside Eusebius, who had gripped the back of the saddle.

'Damn nice morning,' said Eusebius.

'A terror,' said Tarry.

'Well?' said Eusebius with meaning.

'Damn to the thing doing, Eusebius,' said Tarry.

'Be jabus! did you see her?'

'I did. She has no fella as far as I know.'

The two young men were talking about girls. Ninety per cent of their conversation was about girls. Only talk. Always talk. They were idealists and always very lonely. Something had gone wrong with the machinery of living and nothing they ever planned in this line ever came to anything.

They were both more than twenty-seven in those enthusiastic years of nineteen hundred and thirty-five, yet neither had as much as ever kissed a girl. Not that kissing was much in favour in that district. Reading about lovers kissing, Tarry often reflected on the fact that he had never seen anyone kissing anyone, except poor old Peter Toole whom he once saw kissing a corpse in a wakehouse in the hope of getting a couple of glasses of whiskey.

Tarry loved all nice young girls. He loved virtuous girls, and that was one of the things he admired the Catholic religion for – because it kept girls virtuous until such time as he'd meet them.

Tarry was not bad looking, and up to a point he was a great favourite with women. Once a girl in a dance hall called him 'an oul' monk'. The last thing he wanted to be was an oul' monk, and in his heart the last thing he was. Beneath the crust was the too soft heart of a romantic idealist. He had written some verses at that time, too, but these poems did not jut out of his life to become noticeable or make him a stranger to the small farmer community of which he was a child. Eusebius shared most of Tarry's views on everything; for Eusebius was a product of that semi-human Gaelic enthusiasm which had swept the country in his father's day. Eusebius had caught the contagion from an uncle and he had a sentimental regard for poetry – especially the poetry of Mangan and translations of Gaelic poems such as Callanan had done. One of his favourite pieces was Mangan's *Nameless One*, in which he saw the reflection of his own loneliness and lack of female companionship.

> I saw her once one little while and then no more,
> Twas Paradise on earth awhile and then no more.

'Did you hear anything about the other thing, Tarry? – no developments?'

'Heard she went to the Big Man about it.'

'Holy God! To Father Daly?'

'She was seen going up to the Parochial.'

Eusebius jerked his shoulders somewhat hysterically and giggled, 'There'll be sport about this, there'll be sport about this.'

'They can go to hell,' was all Tarry said.

Near the village they came up with the last Mass-goers. Down the Mass-path that served the hilly part of the parish two old women were coming. 'That's like your mother,' Tarry remarked.

They left the bicycle among the other bicycles against the wall of the graveyard and, while Tarry took the clips off his trousers, still kept running along so that their hop-and-go-constant gait was like the progress of kangaroos or horses with itch in the heels. Every one, who till he came within sight of the chapel was in no hurry at all, suddenly developed that anxiety which will be noticed among people who, approaching a football field, hear across the paling the first cheers or the referee's whistle. Tarry, too, was infected.

Tarry and Eusebius were of one mind now in hoping that the man with the collecting box would have left the chapel door. Passing the forge they saw Charlie Trainor's old mother looking for two ha'pennies for a penny, and though they thought her mean they themselves never gave even a ha'penny at the door. Indeed they could not very well afford a ha'penny, for cigarettes and dances and an occasional Saturday evening in the town required every penny and ha'penny they could rap or run.

The man with the collecting box, luckily enough, was disappearing round the gable of the chapel on his way to the sacristy with the takings as they came up the incline through the graveyard to the chapel door.

The Catholic Church of Dargan was a building like a barn – a common rectangle, with a square belfry at the north gable; the church was scaling its mortar rough-casting and its pink wash was almost faded white. The roof span was wide and the roof timbers rotten so that only people with a strong faith in God's goodness-to-His-own would risk sitting in the centre aisle. The centre aisle was always packed, which proved that both faith and piety abided in the parish of Dargan. Standing on a rise in the middle of a weedy graveyard above the village with its shops and new dance hall the church looked shabby, but God would surely overlook this apparent disrespect in the blaze of the people's devotion. There were faith and piety and all the richness of human character that goes with a deep faith in the Hereafter. Father Daly said First Mass on the Feast of Corpus Christi. The chapel was crowded, for as well as being a Feast Day of importance, on which the Faithful were exhorted to receive Holy Communion, this day was also the big summer fair day in the neighbouring town, and many of the congregation had business in the town and by coming to early Mass were able to serve both God and Mammon. The doors and windows were open, but still the place was stuffy with that morning closeness which comes before people are acclimatized to summer. Outside the door a group of men stood whispering while the less solemn parts of the Mass were being said. These men stared about them at the rolling country of little hills and commented on the crops, the weather, the tombstones or whatever came into their dreaming minds.

'Very weedy piece of spuds, them of Mick Finnegan's.'

'He doesn't put on the dung, Larry: the man that doesn't drive on the dung won't take out a crop.' A pause, 'Nothing like the dung.'

'Give me your cap till I kneel on it,' someone said with a laugh.

'All the kneeling you'll do, Charlie . . .'

John Magan, the puce-faced publican, and his flat-footed wife were coming up the incline. The men at the door made way for them and Charlie Trainor the calf-dealer, who was kneeling on one knee with his eye to a chink in the half-open door, gave the big man a quick salute with his upraised fingers.

'I say, quit the bloody spitting on my boot,' someone growled to his neighbours.

Tarry and Eusebius had now arrived and were standing

quietly by the sidewall of the chapel near the door, unobserved. Presently Tarry moved through the crowd in the porch.

'He couldn't see the women from here,' said Charlie.

Tarry ignored their banter and when the Mass Book was being changed for the first Gospel he took advantage of the commotion of the congregation rising to slip in unobserved, except by the young women who made it their business to watch every man as he came in. Tarry disliked staying at the door, not because he had any strong faith or piety, but because he found the atmosphere there annoying. As he edged his way into a place behind a pillar he gave a quick look round the women's side of the chapel. The sexes were on different sides of the Dargan chapel. The congregation was in danger of becoming squint-eyed owing to this arrangement. Even plain women look pretty in a church. As he knelt down after the Creed he leaned on the back of the seat before him and through the crook of his arm surveyed the priest and the people. He had neither prayer book nor rosary beads, nor any other devotional pass-the-time.

It was a squalid grey-faced throng. The sunlight through the coloured windows played on that congregation but could not smooth parchment faces and wrinkled necks to polished ivory. Skin was the colour of clay, and clay was in their hair and clothes. The little tillage fields went to Mass. No wonder that Father Daly had such a low opinion of his parishioners. When he first came to the parish he said there was only one decent man in the whole place and that was the publican – with the miller a bad second. Decency referred in this connection to the size of the property and not to the character of the individual. In the heat the drone the ceremony and the hum of the prayer sounded like an airplane hovering in the distance, or a wasp at the window. Father Daly was a fine cut of a man; he had been educated at Rome and Louvain and was full of a pedantic scholasticism which he somehow managed to relate to the needs of the people. When he left this acquired pedantry at home and took on to speak on politics or economics, which he often did, he made himself look silly. But never to the people. The people of Dargan thought him the loveliest and best educated priest in the diocese and even Tarry

14

Flynn in moments of excitement conceded that the man was above the average country priest. When he turned round to preach, the congregation sat up and admired his fine-shaped head, his proud bearing and his flashing green eyes behind the rimless glasses on which the sun was playing.

He had a silvery voice, so that even nonsense from him sounded wise. He took out a white silk handkerchief from the folds of his chasuble and wiped his glasses. Then he made a dramatic gesture with the fluttering handkerchief before blowing his nose with a loud report like a motor horn. Father Daly was up to every stage trick and would have made an excellent Hyde Park speaker. When (as happened on this Sunday) he had something important to say he usually led up to it by a cleverly constructed runway of philosophy, so that his listeners would be wondering what he was coming at. They knew his ways and his tricks and when, on this occasion, he started off, not with a philosophical but a poetical theme, they guessed that something interesting was in the air. 'There was a great poet one time,' he began, slowly, and in a minor key, 'and his name was Tom Moore. He wrote a song called *Rich and Rare*. "Rich and rare were the gems she wore —"' The priest spoke solemnly, enunciating every word separately. Then he blew his nose again, and as his eyes swept the corners of the chapel his glasses flashed on the walls and were spots of light in the mirroring glass of the Stations of the Cross.

'Rich and rare were the gems she wore
And a bright gold ring on her wand she bore;
But O her beauty was far beyond
Her sparkling gem and snow-white wand.

Lady, dost thou not fear to stray
So lone and lovely on this bleak way?
Are Erin's sons so good or so cold
As not to be tempted by woman or gold?

Sir Knight, I fear not the least alarm,
No son of Erin would offer me harm.
For though they love women and golden store,
Sir Knight, they love honour and virtue more.'

15

Father Daly took his time with the verses, and he spoke so well, and his words seemed the prelude to so much that not even the greediest man for the world, waiting to go to the fair, nor the Communicant with the thickest fasting-spit was annoyed.

The priest stared into the distance as he said: 'That couldn't be said by a lady passing through the village or parish of Dargan today. No, it could not,' he sighed. He raised his voice to a roar that quivered the rafters and echoed in the galleries. 'Rapscallions of hell, curmudgeons of the devil that are less civilized than the natives on the banks of the Congo. Like a lot of pigs that you were after throwing cayenne pepper among?' The people opened their eyes wider and listened, leaning forward – delighted with the sermon. The men at the door came into the porch and Charlie Trainor peeped through a chink in the woodwork. 'Come to hell outa that or he'll see you,' someone warned him.

'Everything's game ball,' Charlie said, and winked.

'Hypocrites, humbugs,' the priest went on, 'coming here Sunday after Sunday – blindfolding the devil in the dark as the saying goes. And the headquarters of all this rascality is a townland called Drumnay.' The congregation smiled. Tarry Flynn stooped his head and smiled, too, although he was a native of that terrible townland. The calf-dealer at the door cocked his ear more acutely; he too, was interested in his townland and pleased when its evil deeds got the air.

'A young girl was passing through this village the other evening,' said the priest sorrowfully. 'She was riding her bicycle home from Confession. When she was passing Drumnay crossroads she was set upon by a crowd of blackguards – and blackguards is no name for them – and the clothes torn off her back. Good God, good God, what is this country coming to? Atheists, scallywags ...' Then relaxing the intensity of his passionate outburst he continued softly, 'I don't blame the unfortunate wretches so much, but I do blame the half-educated blackguards who put them up to such work – the men who make the balls for others to fire.' What was he driving at? Who was the girl? What really happened? The ordinary members of the congregation took the priest's words with a grain of humorous salt and peasant doubt, knowing what wonders Church and State can make out of the common affairs of life when seen in their official mirror. Somebody winked across at Tarry Flynn, who sat with his head bowed and the pleasant smile on his face being thrown to the shadows between the seats. Charlie Trainor never smiled when the priest was preaching; he kept peeping through the woodwork, taking everything in with a serious look.

The respectable people, like the police and the stationmaster and the schoolteachers, and the miller and the publican and his wife all put on mouths of righteousness and narrowed eyes. This was not good enough in a Catholic country. This was not good enough for County Cavan in the year nineteen hundred and thirty-five. And the men leading the revolt against decency and authority were Tarry Flynn and Eusebius Cassidy. Weren't they the two ends of hypocrites coming to Mass the same as decent men? Should be chased to hell out of the parish. And that whole bunch of half-chewed idiots from Drumnay, they weren't so bad if fellows like these didn't come putting ideas into their heads. And Charlie Trainor, that was another prize boy. But *he* would never do any harm so long as he was doing well at his business. But the other pair, they were the right blackguards. So thought respectability. 'I'll not rest or relax,' the priest concluded, 'till I make an example of these scoundrels who are sullying the fair name of this parish. I'll bring them to the bar of justice if it takes me ten years. Yes, Drumnay cross-roads where a decent man or woman can't pass without a clod being thrown at them or some nasty expression. They come here to Mass and they were better at home – a thousand times better.' The priest broke off suddenly and began to read out a list of notices, including one that a grand carnival dance would be held in the hall on that same evening, the charge for admission – gentlemen three-and-six, ladies half-a-crown. And furthermore, the right of admission should be strictly reserved. Tarry had an attack of conscience. When the priest turned away to face the Altar he knelt with his chin on the heels of his shut fists and a faraway look of childhood piety in his eyes.

Outside the chapel the little knots of the congregation picking up their homing companions hardly mentioned the sermon. There were other more urgent things to fill their minds – the crops and the fair and their neighbours.

Even Mrs Flynn, who was standing by her yard gate with the two baskets of cocks ready to move off to the railway station, had no time to discuss the scandal. Tarry had expected her to go into terrible tantrums when he got home and was pleasantly surprised at her temper.

'That cow is not looking at the bull, thank God,' she said. It was probably this that put her in good humour.

Tarry helped her with the baskets of cocks the short distance to the railway halt.

'Take off that good suit,' she advised her son, 'and not have everything on the one rack like the Carlins, and give Aggie a hand with the dinner.'

Tarry promised to do as advised.

The quiet time between the two Masses on Sundays and holy-days was for Tarry the happiest time of his life – especially when all the rest of the household was at second Mass and he was in sole control. He could read and smoke his fill without his mother's interruptions. His mother disliked his reading and smoking far more than any of his other habits.

He washed the potatoes for the dinner in the tub before the door and put on the ten-gallon pot.

Then sitting by the fire, keeping it stoked, he sat smoking and reading the *Messenger*. The *Messenger of the Sacred Heart* was bought every month, and with *Old Moore's Almanac* and the local newspaper constituted the literature of Flynn's as of nearly every other country house.

Flynn's house had the reputation of being possessed of some wonderful books. Tarry's father, who died some years previously, had an interest in books and had bought several second-hand volumes in the market of the local town. His books were not very exciting, but they *were* books. A gazetteer for the year 1867, an antiquated treatise on Sound, Light and Heat, and a medical book called *Thompson's Domestic Medicine*.

18

The only one of the three which Tarry had ever known father to read was the 'doctor's book'. His father had taken a few prescriptions out of it for the common illnesses of his friends. Once he gave a prescription for jaundice to a man which must have worked; for from that day to the day he died the father had the reputation of having a traditional cure for the jaundice and men and women came from far and near for the 'cure'.

Tarry had no books except these and a couple of school readers. One was a famous Sixth Book which he had stolen from a neighbour's house some years before. It was in this book he got all the poetry he knew.

He could read anything, so hungry was he for reading. So he read the *Messenger*, all of it from the verses by Brian O'Higgins on the Sacred Heart – a serial poem which ran for a year or more – to the story of the good young girl who had a vocation, and who was being sabotaged by the bad man, right through to the Thanksgivings 'for favours received', at the back.

The sunlight came in through the dusty window, making a magical sunbeam right across the kitchen.

Aggie had gone to the well for water.

When she came in she offered to keep an eye on the pot and not let it boil all over the floor. She had also to see that the delicate chicken who was rolled up in a black stocking in a porringer by the hob did not get scalded or burned.

In the midst of this beautiful repose there was a great hen flutter in the street and brother and sister both rushed out. It was the hawk of course, but as far as they could see he had got nothing.

Tarry put the *Messenger* in his pocket and climbed Callan's Hill, a favourite climb of his.

Walking backwards up its daisied slope he gazed across the valley right across to the plains of Louth, and gazing he dreamed into the past.

O the thrilling daisies in the sun-baked hoof-tracks. O the wonder of dry clay. O the mystery of Eternity stretching back is the same as its mystery stretching forward.

That was Tarry: Eternity and Earth side by side.

19

Suddenly his mind came back to the precise particulars of the immediate scene. Drumnay –

Drumnay was a long crooked valley zig-zagging West-East between several ranges of hills in Cavan. The valley part of it was mostly cut-away bog, so that the only arable land was a thin stripe along the bottom of the hills and the hills themselves. It is not to be wondered at that the minds of the natives were shaped by and like the environment. In cul-de-sac pocket valleys all the way up the length of the townland were other smaller farms, inaccessible, and where the owners were inclined to be frustrated and, so, violent. At the western end of the valley Flynn's comfortable farmhouse stood. The poplar-lined lane that served the townland branched off the main road about two hundred yards from the Flynn homestead. With the whitethorn hedges in full leaf the road seemed no more to one looking across country than a particularly thick hedge.

Tarry sat on the crown of the hill with his back to a bank of massed primroses and violets, and as he sat there the heavy slumberous time and place made him forget the sting of the thorn of a dream in his heart. Why should a man want to climb out of this anonymous happiness in the conscious day?

Cassidy's field of oats was doing very well. A beautiful green field of oats. He was a bit jealous of the oats, and doubted if his own was doing as well. He stared into the hazy blue distance and heard the puff-puff of a train coming in through the boggy hollows five miles away. The earth under him trembled.

'Tarry, Tarry, Tarry!'

His sister's cry recalled him to reality.

'What?' he shouted down.

'Come down and give us a hand to teem the pot.'

Wasn't that a nuisance? Just when he was beginning to be happy something like this always disturbed him.

As he was coming down the hill the first people on bicycles were coming from second Mass – his two sisters amongst them. His next-door neighbour, May Callan, was with them. May was one of the girls with whom he was in love. She was reality. But nothing was happening after all his spring daydreams. The land keeps a man silent for a generation or two and then the crust gives way. A poet is born or a prophet.

Teeming the pot into a bucket, he put a sack apron around him, and holding one of the legs of the pot with his right hand and the pot lid with his left he drained off the water.

Even teeming the pot was very important in his life and in his imagination. Any incident, or any act, can carry within it the energy of the imagination.

Outside at the gate he could hear his other two sisters in loud giggling conversation with May.

As soon as he had the pot teemed he found an excuse to wander in the direction of the girls so as not to make the overture seem too deliberate. He pulled the saddle-harrow out from where it lay against the low wall before the house with a very concerned air. All the time he was trying to impress his personality on May. But it was no use. He could not understand why he was ignored by young women, for he knew he was attractive.

Could it be that girls knew that beneath his poetic appearance was primitive savagery and lust? In his innocence that was his surmise then. So he put on yet a further coat of apparent virtue. This made the situation worse, but he did not notice the worsening.

His own sisters, too, treated him with little respect. One day he struck Aggie with his open palm and knocked her across the kitchen floor – and curiously enough, from that day forward she was the only one who deferred to his masculinity.

With women in general he was truthful and sincere and would talk philosophy or Canon Law (Canon Law fascinated him, though what he knew of the subject was utter nonsense) to them on the slightest provocation. Women cannot understand honesty in a man.

He carefully replaced the saddle-harrow and walked to the gate and glanced down the lane.

'... so he said "me hand on yer drawers" says he, and says she ... What the bleddy hell are ye listening to women's talk for?' It was Bridie who was speaking. May was looking at Tarry with cold indifference, as he thought.

'The birds of Angus,' he said in a dramatically silly tone.

Tarry had a number of meaningless phrases which he used to astonish girls with. This particular phrase he had read somewhere. By saying something queer like this he expected to get the attention of the mystery-loving heart of woman. Women thought him a little touched when he made such remarks. This was not the arcanum to which they were accustomed. He knew it was not the usual aphrodisiacal double-meaning, illiterate joking which a man such as Charlie Trainor was an adept at, but he felt that it ought to be much more effective. It wasn't.

And so the girls at the gate separated and Tarry was left – with his dreams.

He couldn't go to the town that day, because his two sisters, Aggie and Bridie, were going in the hope of getting a man, and he had to keep an eye on things. It was dangerous to leave a small farm without a steward for a day. Something was liable to go wrong, and then there would be a row with his mother. So all day he had plenty of time to read and smoke. Getting enough money to buy cigarettes was a problem; if it wasn't for all the eggs he stole and which Aggie sold for him he'd be without a cigarette many a time.

The day passed.

Cyclists passed down the lane on their way to the town. The bawl of unsold cattle could be heard as they were being driven home. Tarry was not unhappy.

Tarry was running a centre in the potato drills. As he was using only one horse to pull the old plough the work was rather bumpy – and in the local phrase 'in and out like a dog pissing on snow'.

Was he interested very deeply in his work? In some ways, yes. Although he was trying to compose a verse as he worked he was also thinking with much comfort of the excellent progress his potatoes were making. They were three inches over the tops of the drills, the best spuds in the country. Growing potatoes was a thing he took a great pride in. By merely admiring the buds as they grew he felt that they responded and progressed. Indeed he was sure they responded. Clay climbed in the back of his boots.

The plough struck a rock and the handles flew high over his shoulders. Up and down the alleys he went for about an hour in a great hurry. Then he sat on the beam of the plough to dream.

As he dreamt Molly Brady came down the path on the far side of the dividing stream, towards the well. In one hand she carried a tin can and in the other a long pot-stick. She left the can beside the well and began to search with the pot-stick in the rushes that grew in the swamp; she was looking for hens' nests.

Molly was about twenty years old, a soft, fat slob of a girl who appealed to Tarry in a sensual way.

And for weeks in his daydreams he had been planning an approach to her. He knew the times she'd be coming to the well. Accidental-like he had a large plank lying across the stream for a week or more now – he had it there for the purpose of making a platform when he would be removing the big boulder that had rolled into the stream, blocking the flow of water. Molly's mother did not get up out of bed these mornings until near eleven. That would be a good time. Among his other arrangements he had two large corn sacks which presumably were for covering the horse when he would be cooling down after a sweat. And now the time had arrived.

Molly was obviously waiting for Tarry to open the conversation. It was plain that her interest in the hens' secret nests was merely collateral.

'Hello,' he called.

This 'hello' conveyed a different meaning from other hellos. In country places a single word is inflected to mean a hundred things, so that only a recording of the sounds gives an idea of the speech of these people.

This hello had in it a touch of bravado, the speech of a wicked monster making a bid for a woman's virtue, the consciousness of the wickedness producing a tremulous quality in the tones. Speaking, he felt that the whole countryside was listening to his vile suggestion.

'Hello,' answered Molly. Her hello was a wild animalistic cry.

'Fierce great weather, Molly,' said Tarry, going towards the edge of the stream.

'I'm looking for a nest of oul' eggs,' said Molly with a pout of bitterness which was aimed at some hens unknown, 'and bad luck from the same hens how well it's here they have to come to lay. How's your mother?'

'Damn to the bother, Molly. They wouldn't by any chance be laying on this side of the drain. Do you know what it is, Molly, I kind-a thought I saw one making a nest on this side.'

Molly was standing in the rushes with her legs wide apart and the pot-stick stuck between them, like a witch ready to take off on her broom. Tarry in his mind was crouching nearer his prey. If he could get her out on this side of the stream he would have the battle three-quarters won. But first he had to make his escape sure. If she started to screech what excuse would he make? Would he be able to pass the thing over as a joke?

Suddenly he realized that this game would take hours to develop. The game wasn't worth the trouble. That was it; any man could have any woman provided he was willing to be patient. He decided to put the affair off until some other time. Molly would be liable to be visiting Flynn's house one of these nights and he'd have a better chance if he waited and waylaid her as she went home alone through the meadows.

As he reasoned to himself – sure, good God, a man would be mad to try a thing like that on in the middle of the day.

When Molly went on her way and Tarry was half way up the drill he remembered the technique which always worked in his daydreams. It would work in real life, too, if he had the gumption to put it to the test.

'I'm the two ends of a gulpin,' he said aloud to himself.

And all through that day he kept cursing himself for his cowardice.

At tea-time in Flynn's the mother was chastising Bridie, and Bridie was not behind-hand in replying in similar coinage. The argument which was well under way when Tarry entered, had been started by Bridie, who accused her mother of going about with a face on her like the bottom of a pot.

'Go lang, ye scut, ye,' said the mother, 'how dar ye say a thing like that to me.'

'Oh nobody can talk to you,' said Bridie with a pout, 'if a person only opens their mouth ye ait the face off them.'

'The divil thank ye and thump ye, Bridie, ye whipster, ye. Your face is scrubbed often enough and the damn to the much you're making of it. I could be twice married when I was your age.'

'A wonder ye didn't make a better bargain.'

'Arra what?' the mother was rising in her anger, 'arra what? Is it making little of your poor father – the Lord have mercy on him – ye are? May bad luck to ye into hell and out of it for a tinker that ... Go out one of yez and bring in a lock of sticks for the fire ... Oh a brazen tinker, if ever there was one. Oh a family of daughters is the last of the last. Half of the time painting and powdering and it would take a doctor's shop to keep them in medicine.'

'Will ye shut up.'

'I will not shut up. There's that poor fella there (Tarry) and he didn't get a drop of tay and him tired working in the field all day. Go now and put on the kettle, Bridie, and make him his tay.'

'He'll die, poor chap, if he doesn't get his tay. Nothing for the mother here only the big fella. There's no talk of making tay for us when we come in. And we're doing more than him.'

'What are yez doing? what are yez doing? I don't see much of your work ... How did ye get on the day, Tarry?'

'Nearly finished.'

'Ye shouldn't try to do a bull-dragging day. Isn't there more days than years. Listen, listen.' They all listened to the rattle of the road gate. 'I hope to the sweet and honourable father,' gasped Mrs Flynn, 'that it's not someone coming in on top of us at this hour of the evening. Whip that kettle off the fire and not have us making tay for him.'

Aggie took off the kettle, shoved it under the stairs and disarranged the clean tea-mugs on the table. The mother dashed to the door. It was Mrs Callan prowling for her ducks, which were laying out those nights.

'Won't ye come in and rest your stockings, Mrs Callan?' Mrs Flynn said, with enthusiastic hospitality.

'I can't till I get me ducks,' she said in her sneaky crying voice.

'Would ye let me look into your stable to see if they might be there? I thought I saw them coming this way.'

Mrs Flynn did not like the suggestion that she was exploiting Callan's ducks. Indeed this was not the first time that Mrs Callan had come round on a similar errand.

'Troth, the only time, Mrs Callan,' said Mrs Flynn, 'that you'd be sure of finding your ducks about our street is when we're feeding the hens. They are the boys for aiting me hens' feeding, Mrs Callan, but as for dropping an egg here that's the last thing they'd think of. Oh, catch them to lay about a stranger's place.'

'It's a wonder they'd be coming, then, to ait your hens' feeding seeing that they have the run of the fields and the bog – the two bogs at that.'

'Troth, there's damn all nourishment in the fields or in the bogs, Mrs Callan. If that's all ducks get the devil the many eggs they'll lay.' Tarry went to the road gate to see if his neighbour Eusebius was coming.

The mother called him: 'Tarry, did ye chance to see Mrs Callan's ducks knocking about this evening?'

'They were over in our field trying to look for worms in the drills after me about three hours ago. After that I saw them making for Cassidy's field of oats.'

'Aren't they the terrible travellers,' Mrs Callan drawled innocently. 'It must be the breed.'

'Troth,' said Mrs Flynn, 'it's the breed of everything to look for the full of their bellies, Mrs Callan. The ducks will always come home if they're sure of getting a feed when they come.'

When Mrs Callan was gone Mrs Flynn turned to her son: 'That party never fed man or baste in their life. Even the cats come here and I often take pity on them mewing for a sup of milk. Mane lot of beggars and the consait of them. Why, that young whipster of theirs, May, you'd think she was the lady of the land. With her little black head and her sparrow-legs, ach, she's not a girl nor a patch on a girl's backside ... Gwan, now, hen, into the house with ye.' The woman shooed the wandering hen in the direction of the hen-house door. 'I don't like a hen that doesn't go to roost early in the evening; she won't lay the next day. My, isn't it a lovely warm evening.' She gazed up the valley.

'Is that Petey Meegan I see? Another slack gelding. The devil the woman he'll ever take now.'

2

The silly attack on the girl at the cross-roads, though it was a fairly ordinary occurrence, appeared to have set Father Daly thinking – thinking that life in Dargan was in danger of boiling over in wild orgies of lust. And what did he decide to do but make arrangements for a big Mission to the parishioners by the Order of Redemptorists who were such specialists in sex sins.

Nothing could have appeared more pathetic to Tarry or Eusebius when the news got around. The parish was comprised of old unmarried men and women. For a mile radius from where Flynn's lived Tarry could only count four houses in which there were married couples with children.

From a devotion known as the Nine Fridays, Tarry was able to assess the number of old maids in the parish, for this devotion – which he had in his childhood practised – was the old unmarried girl's escape from the fruitless flower of virginity. On the first Friday of every month these old girls could be seen strolling home from the village church, their sharp tongues in keeping with their sharp noses. Tarry, when he reflected on this devotion, was glad that he had gone through it, for there was a story that anyone who had done so would never die unrepentant. That gave a man a great chance to have a good time.

The crooked old men sat up and took notice when they heard of the Mission; they began to dream themselves violent young stallions who needed prayer and fasting to keep them on the narrow path.

Mrs Flynn was glad to hear of the Mission too.

'I hope this'll stir up the pack of good-for-nothing geldings that's on the go in Dargan. And you'll have to go too,' she said to her son.

Petey Meegan from Miskin, across the hills, passing Flynn's house was in wonderful humour.

'I believe that the two men that's coming are the two toughest men in the Order,' said he, and his eyes began to dance under his bleary eyelids.

Old maids like Jennie Toole coming around were filled with the tales of awful things that young men had done to girls in that parish. 'It takes out,' she said to Mrs Flynn. She told how a certain girl was raped and another one half raped, while Mrs Flynn clicked her tongue, not looking at all displeased.

It was a story of life in a townland of death.

As far as Tarry could gather from his mother's talk about the Mission, she had hopes that the Missioners' condemnation of sex would have the effect of drawing attention to it.

He was paring her corn this morning before going out to finish the moulding of the potatoes when she said: 'It might stir them up ... Easy now and don't draw blood. You'd never know the good it might do. I was talking to one of the McArdles there and I was telling him that he ought to be getting a woman. "Huh," says he, "what would I be doing with a woman? I have me pint and me fag," says he, "and I'm not going to bring in a woman." You ought to hurry with the praties before the ground gets too dry.'

He moulded the potatoes that day, his mind lifted to a new excitement by the thought of all the strange girls that would be coming to the Mission. It often worried him that a lot of other men might be as hypocritical as himself. He, when he analysed himself, knew that he went to religious events of this kind mainly to see the girls.

The clay was running through his mind.

He gloated over his potatoes and the fine job he was making of the moulding, though he was only using one horse. The clay was staying up nicely.

Molly came to the well several times that day but he was too engrossed in his work to take much notice of her.

The Holy Ghost was taking the Bedlam of the little fields and making it into a song, a simple song which he could understand. And he saw the Holy Spirit on the hills.

With the cynical side of himself, he realized that there was

29

nothing unusual about the landscape. And yet what he imagined was hardly self-deception. The totality of the scene about him was a miracle. There might be something of self-deception in his imagination of the general landscape but there was none in his observation of the little flowers and weeds. These had God's message in them.

Filled with <u>mystical thoughts</u> he loosed out the horse that evening, threw the backrope and traces on the beam of the plough and let the mare out on the grass, and then went home to try out his ideas on his mother. In moments like these he was rapt to the silly heavens. Often, as now, he only said outlandish things to his mother to test them. Anything that stood up to her test would stand up to anything.

'Did you get finished?' said she.

'I did,' he said. He organized his will for a remarkable statement. 'The Holy Spirit is in the fields,' he said in even cold tones. He was unemotional, for these strange statements did not lend themselves to any human emotion.

The mother who had one shoe off and her foot on a stool did not seem to have heard. 'There's a curse o' God corn on that wee toe and it's starting to bother me again. I think we'll have a slash of rain. Get the razor blade and pare it for me.' He held the foot between his legs like a blacksmith shoeing a horse. 'Easy now,' she cried, 'and don't draw blood. Easy now, easy now. The Mission's opening next Sunday week, I hear. Aggie, run out and don't leave any feeding on the hens' dishes for Callan's ducks. Have you the pea out?'

'I have.'

After a while she quietly asked:

'What was that you said about the Holy something?'

'I said the Holy Spirit was in the fields.'

'Lord protect everyone's rearing,' she said with a twinkle that was half humorous and half terror in her eye. She knew that there was no madness on her side of the house – that was one sure five – but –

'Is it something to do with the Catholic religion you mean?'

'It has to do with every religion; it's beauty in Nature,' he said solemnly but also dispassionately.

30

It was a mad remark but it was said by a very sane man.

'You'll have to go to this Mission every evening, Tarry. I don't want to have the people talking, and it's talking they'd be. The last time there was a Mission in this parish ...' She put her finger to her lip and began to consider ... 'How many years ago would that be? It's either ten or eleven ... the devil a go the Carlins ever went and their luck wasn't much the better of it ... Did you scrape the dishes clane, Aggie? Oh, they had the devil's luck. You made a great job of that corn. I hadn't a foot to put under me.'

Tarry was moving out the door.

'And they couldn't have luck, people like them ...'

He went as far as the road gate and returned.

'Are you back?' said the mother.

He was hoping to get some money for cigarettes but he said: 'I thought I left something here,' and he searched under the papers in the back window.

'Don't be throwing the *Messenger* on the ground and me not having it read,' said Aggie.

'It's rubbish.'

'That's the class of a man Tarry is,' said Aggie, 'always making little of religion.'

'I only said that the writing, the stories, in it were no good, that's all I said.'

'I suppose you'd take on to write better ones.'

'You keep your mouth shut, Aggie,' said the mother. 'But for God's sake and for everyone's sake don't let anyone outside hear you saying these things,' she addressed her son. 'The people that's going in this place are only waiting for the chance to carry stories to the Parochial House – like what happened over the Reilly one. What in the Name of the three gay fellas *are* you pouching for?'

'For nothing, I tell you.'

'There's a shilling there on the dresser and you can take it,' she said at last, 'but try and not to spend it. I like a man to have money in his pocket.'

He went out singing. The shilling made all the difference between a man who hated the parish and a lover of it.

Every evening himself and Eusebius went down the road, but since the stallion season opened Eusebius was disinclined to go too far away from the mouth of the Drumnay road lest he should miss a customer with a mare.

On this evening Tarry met his neighbour outside when he went to the gate the second time and together they walked slowly down the road.

'I'm going to ask you a thing I often had a mind to ask you before,' Tarry started out of nowhere, and puffed away at the long cigarette which he had the cunning to have lighted before Eusebius came on the scene.

'Yes?' said Eusebius with indifference, for he was listening for the distant sounds of neighing mares.

'Had you ever anything to do with a woman, Eusebius?'

'Good God, no.'

'Can I take that for the God's honest truth?'

'To be sure, man.'

Tarry was very much relieved to think of one man at least being so moral. Every moral man meant one rival less for him. Having satisfied himself as to the truth of Eusebius' reply he turned to other matters, and in a short time they were deep in the question of the moulding of the potatoes.

So the days went by and the corn grew taller and shot out, the potato-stalks closed the alleys and the turnips softened over the dry clay. And the Mission came round.

Every able-bodied man and woman in the parish was present at the opening of the Mission. Looking across the church Tarry and Eusebius, who were together, thought they never saw so many grey-headed and bald-headed men in one bunch, and all of them so alike in many ways. The same stoop, the same slightly roguish look in every eye, the look of old blackguards who are being flattered by bawdy suggestions; the same size generally and even similar sort of clothes. On the women's side of the church huddled as intense a crowd of barren virgins as had ever gathered together at the same time in that parish.

Up in the galleries there was a spattering of young girls and visitors from the local parishes and towns, but these could not lessen the terrible impact of the old bachelors and maids in the body of the church.

The two most passionate preachers in the Redemptorist Order in Dundalk had been called in to give the Mission. One of these made a tremendous sermon that evening. As it registered in Tarry's mind it was all about a boy who met a girl and as a result of the boy's behaviour the girl committed suicide. She was found in a well. And the preacher said with a cry that would tear the heart out of a stone: 'That man damned that girl's soul.'

For all its passion the sermon left Tarry indifferent. Compared to one of Father Daly's sermons it lacked that touch of humour, that appearance of not being too earnest, which is the real sign of sincerity.

The second Missioner was hearing Confessions during the sermon and the transformation he was effecting in the minds of the penitents was astonishing. Men who had forgotten what they were born for came out of the confessional, in the words of Charlie Trainor, 'ready to bull cows'. This was the effect the Mission was having on all minds.

Outside the church there were stalls set up where gay-coloured Rosaries and wild red religious pictures and statues were for sale. The women who owned these stalls were fantastic dealing women with fluent tongues and a sense of freedom which was unknown in Dargan. They were bohemians who had an easy manner with God – like poets or actresses.

Life was beginning in Dargan.

The sticky clay began to fall away from Tarry's feet and as he went home one evening with Eusebius he suggested that they should take a run round Dillons, 'just for a cod'. The Dillons did not attend the Mission, but they must have liked it, for it provided them with new opportunities. When all the parish was at the Mission service in the evening they could almost do what they liked in the green fields along the road. Charlie set out to go to the Mission but it seemed that he went no farther than Dillon's house.

Ahead of Tarry and his neighbour walked the groups of old men and the lines of old maids. The conversation of the men was excited, even though they were talking about football and the big match that was being held in the village on the following Sunday.

'Should be a desperate gate, Hughie.'

'Twenty pound.'

'If it 'ill be trusting to it.'

And so on.

The women were gossiping about their hens, and some of the most hopeless old maids were discussing with sharp horror the doings of the Dillons. And everyone seemed to be going somewhere now, going somewhere with a purpose.

Dillon's house was a thatched cottage about a hundred yards in off the main road, half way between Dargan and Drumnay. The path up to the house continued as a short-cut across the hills which was used by the natives of Miskin and sometimes by the people of Drumnay. Seen from the road the house was a gay little house, trim, whitewashed, the real traditional Irish cabin.

The two boys without saying anything to each other both decided to take the short-cut. A couple of straggling old women looked after them as if taking notice and wondering why they were going that way. For once in his life Tarry felt no guilty conscience. He was pleasantly hysterical like a young girl at a wedding.

They were not talking about girls now:

'I put clay up to me spuds last week,' said Tarry, 'and they're doing terribly well.'

'The potash is your man,' said Eusebius.

'I only put on the bare hundred,' said Tarry, boastful of the soil of his farm.

'You did and the rest,' said Eusebius, but he was not thinking of potatoes.

'Stop a second,' said Tarry in a whisper.

They were standing still, surveying the corner of the field at the bottom of McArdle's hill in Miskin.

'It's him,' said Tarry.

'Isn't he the two ends of a hure?' said Eusebius.

Charlie was the man who was sneaking along the hedge in that corner, and the girl with him was Josie Dillon.

'As sure as there's an eye in a hawk,' said Eusebius.

'We'll watch him,' said Tarry.

When they came to the gable of Dillon's house they could see across the low boxwood hedge the little flower garden before the door, with rings of beautiful flowers. Around the doors and windows grew roses, wildish white roses and cream ones and red ones. And from within the house came the sound of laughter.

One of the girls came to the door and emptied the tea-pot. As she did so she managed to keep in touch with the conversation within. Those within were the older generations whose desires had come to rest. These did frequent the church, but were not vital in the local life, for nobody would consider them as capable of morality or immorality no more than they would the farm animals. They were looked upon as a people apart, and what they did did not reflect on the life of the ordinary people. There was a great-great grandmother in the house, the only great-great grand-mother of the human race that Tarry had ever seen. There would have been a long line of her descendants if they hadn't been con-sumptive. There was a far-out relationship between the Dillons and the Reillys, and some people tried to make out that the Flynns had a drop of the same blood, but Tarry had proved to his own satisfaction that that relationship was no nearer than seventh cousin, and when he declared to the old men of the area that if all the seventh cousins were counted they would include every man, woman and child in Dargan and a lot more outside it, that kept the relationship theory from being developed.

While Tarry was taking in the beauty of the flowers, Eusebius had gone behind the house and peeped in the window.

'Jabus, do you know what?' he said, returning. 'I never saw such a house, shining like a kitten's eye, man, plates on the dresser and everything. Hell of a crowd in there drinking tay and porter. It's a dread.'

'Many of the younger ones in?'

'Only Mary.'

'My God!' Tarry sighed.

He had been developing a sort of pity for two of the youngest girls aged about thirteen and fifteen and he felt that these could be saved if taken in time. But if they couldn't be saved the next best thing would be for him to have them while they were virgins. He didn't tell his mind to Eusebius but led off with a few remarks to get the man's outlook.

'Would you say the two young ones are still all right, Eusebius?'

'How, like?'

'Would you say they had ever men with them?'

They had crossed the stile and were now coming up to one of Kerley's fields. They had to search for a hole in the hedge through which to pass, for apparently the old short-cut had been changed since last they went that way. They had to walk all along the field till they came to the railway. Eusebius was sampling the paling wire instead of replying to his companion's question. 'A few strands of that would come in very useful for fixing a cracked shaft of a cart,' said he.

A head bobbed up from among the long grass on the railway slope, and Tarry, knowing that they were running into the Dillons and their boy friends, urged on Eusebius to come away. He didn't want to see the two young ones with old blackguards. So long as he had some doubts about it he would have an escape but once he was sure – Eusebius didn't understand this at all.

'When we came this far – '

'There may be men waiting with mares for you to come back, Eusebius.'

'They'll know I'm at the Mission and wait. Come on, man.'

'Take your time a minute,' Tarry said, while he considered.

A girl's scream came from the direction of the railway bridge and Tarry's heart was shaken. None of the older Dillon girls would have screamed like that. He was late. He thought the worst. One virgin less for him to dream about.

Eusebius wouldn't wait any longer. He wanted, he said, to see what Charlie was up to, and he dashed down the railway slope and out of sight, calling on Tarry to come on as he disappeared under the long weeds and grass.

Tarry went home alone.

He hadn't the courage on this occasion, but he had plans. In matters of this description a man should plan ahead. No use rushing into something for which he might be sorry. Some other evening he would stay at home from the Mission and make a proper examination of conditions on the railway slope.

He went home in despair.

The mother was making tea when he arrived.

'You were born at meal time,' she said. 'I didn't expect you home yet awhile. I got a lift in Jemmy Kerley's trap – the devil must have broken a rib in him, for he's the narrow-gutted article, a bad garry that doesn't believe in putting too much weight on his springs. Who were you home with?'

'Nobody at all,' he said.

He went upstairs to his room to lie on his bed and read poems from one of the school books. He was looking for something that would console him about lost women, but the best he could find was a lyric by Byron.

> We'll go no more a roving
> So late into the night
> Though the heart be still as loving
> And the moon be still as bright.

He read, and as he read he was not reading the poem as if it were the work of another man: he had written that poem and was now saying it, impressing its romantic meaning on a lonely and beautiful virgin as they walked together then along the primrose bank at the top of Callan's hill.

The Mission was to continue for two weeks. Money was charged going in to it and on the first week all the respectable people had the job of holding the collecting boxes. Tarry had hopes that for the second week he would get one of these honorary jobs, and he went so far as to tell his mother that he didn't fancy the job at all. 'Can't you be like another and do it if you're asked – *if* you're asked. The devil the bit of me thinks you will.'

By the looks of her she would like him to be asked and was only casting doubt upon the suggestion to make the honour more honourable when it came.

On Sunday the curate, Father Markey, read out the list of those who were to hold the boxes and as name after name was announced and still not his, he was getting down-hearted. And when Charlie Trainor's name was announced he could hardly believe his ears. Were the priests blind or did they prefer a man who didn't care a damn for morals one way or the other? It looked very like it.

'You were lucky you wasn't offered one of them oul' jobs,' said Eusebius – who had also been called upon – rubbing the salt in.

'I sent word to Father Markey not to give me out,' Tarry said.

'Oh, I see,' said Eusebius in a manner that damaged Tarry's explanation.

Well, said he to himself one day as he was harnessing the mare in the stable, if they think that little of me I'll not go this evening at all. He stooped down under the belly of the animal to catch the girth strap and as he did he caught a glimpse of the morning sun coming down the valley; it glinted on the swamp and the sedge and flowers caught a meaning for him. That was his meaning. Having found it suddenly, the tying of the girth and the putting of the mare in the cart and every little act became a wonderful miraculous work. It made him very proud too and in some ways impossible. Other important things did not seem important at all.

When his mother came out to give him money for the stuff he was to buy in the shop, his mind was in the clouds.

'Now, don't forget,' said she up to him where he sat on his throne of the seat-board, 'don't forget the salt that I want for the churning.'

'No fear of me to forget,' he said as he took the money.

'I wish I could say that; the last time I sent you for it you forgot; you'd forget your head only it's tied to you. Another thing – if you meet one of them missioners – as you're likely to, for they do be out walking the roads – be nice to him and don't be carrying on with this nonsensical talk that you do be at sometimes ... Mary, go in and keep the pot on the boil ... Now, I'll hear if you say anything.'

38

'Lord God, but you're the innocent woman. Do you think I'd start to talk philosophy to every oul' cod I meet. Go on, mare.'

'Oul' cod, every oul' cod.' Mrs Flynn shook her head in disgust as she closed the gate behind him to keep Callan's straying animals from entering the street. On the way to the village shop he met Father Anthony who was the joker of the Mission. One of the priests sent to a parish was always a 'gay fella'. He cracked a joke on meeting Tarry, and Tarry pulled up. He didn't like this sort of joke when his mind was contemplating the lonely beauty of the landscape around him. He was somewhat abrupt with the monk and in his excitement said the wrong thing: he said the unusual thing, what he had often taken a vow against saying, and that made the monk suspicious. He didn't like to hear originality from a poor farmer and was disappointed to find his well-practised joke treated so indifferently.

Originality showed pride.

'Were you at your Confession yet?' asked the priest.

'I'm well within the walls of the Church,' said Tarry.

'What do you know about the Church?' said the monk a little angrily. 'What has a young country boy like you to do with these things? You must come and let me hear your Confession.'

He asked Tarry his name and where he lived, and finally his age. Asking his age Tarry always found was a sure sign that the man who asked was not friendly. There was always a touch of malice in such a question, it was being familiar. Whenever anyone asked him his age he put him down as an enemy. Considering that he was nearly thirty he would have preferred not being asked. He told the man he was twenty-five. The monk began to chastise Tarry for his outlook and was telling him that he was heading for the downward path when Charlie came by on a bicycle. With a smile like a full moon the monk saluted the calf-dealer and the joke he cracked was warmly enjoyed by Charlie.

Charlie had overheard the missioner's chastisement of Tarry and when they parted with the monk, Charlie, catching hold of the side-board of the cart while still keeping on his bicycle, ran alongside Tarry inquiring what the hell he was saying to the poor missioner.

'You wouldn't know,' said Tarry.

Charlie was very vexed. 'You're a desperate man to be making little of the priests like that, Flynn. We're all Catholics, aren't we?'

'I don't know so much about that, Charlie. Some of us are doubtful.'

'Oh, I see, you don't believe in religion.'

'No, but you do, Charlie,' Tarry sneered.

The way Charlie raised his eyebrows and pretended to be angry made Tarry mad; for he knew that this dishonest attitude was the stuff out of which ignorant bigotry is made. This encounter with the monk and the calf-dealer took most of the good out of his journey to the village which was usually such a pleasant holiday from the drag of his existence.

As he feared, his mother wasn't long hearing about the tiff. She heard it before the day was ended, though she did not accuse him of it till the day after. She talked as if she were terrified, but for all that there was humour in her terror which she couldn't conceal.

'What the devil's father did you say to him?' said she.

'Not one thing.'

'We'll be the talk of the country – like the Carlins. Did you hear that one of the missioners was up with them this evening, trying to get them to come out to the Mission?'

'They're not going?'

'Going, how are you ... Give us up that long potstick from the door ... O, going, aye! And you're taking pattern by them.'

Tarry was disgusted with the Carlins; they were liable to give the impression that having a respect for oneself was a sign of madness. If, in the cause of his self-esteem, *he* stayed at home from the chapel he'd be put down as a queer fellow. Not that he had any intention of missing the carnival spirit that was to be found around the church these days or of revolting against the Church – he had only intended staying away one evening. He would remain away that one evening – and he did. He ran over to the field to take a last look at a heifer that was due to calve and then went down the road as if he were going off to pray. Eusebius had to go off earlier, he being an official.

He crossed the hills into Miskin, intending to come out on the railway line. Passing Petey Meegan's house he saw the crooked old bachelor owner hurrying off up Kerley's hill on his way to hear more about sex.

The shadowy lane with the hedges that nearly met in the middle was filled with midges and flies buzzing over cow-dung. Here he was in another world. It was almost a year since he had gone up that lane and it evoked nostalgia. He remembered as a child coming home from second Mass on Sundays with Eusebius by this lane and how fairylike it seemed to him then. Old Petey's old father used to come out hobbling on his two sticks and like the Ancient Mariner try to get them to listen to his stories of the Sleeping Horsemen who were enchanted under a hill near Ardee. One day they would awaken to fight against the enemies of the Church. It was to be a deadly fight and the time would be the End of the World. There was an apocalyptic flavour about all those stories and the memory of them influenced the heavy-smelling fungi and flowers that grew in the dark ditches.

A great row was going on in McArdle's kitchen.

The four sons were arguing with their father and mother for money. These four sons were all over forty but they were treated as babies by their parents. That may have been why when they appeared at Drumnay cross-roads or in the discussions in Magan's pub they were so aggressive and spoke with airs of such domineering authority.

'I want a shilling for fags and I'll have to get it,' a powerful lamenting voice could be heard.

A pup screamed and ran under the table.

'Am I made of money? Am I made of money?' the father cried.

The mother was now crying quietly and Tarry hurried along, knowing that a family row is a most unhealthy affair for an outsider.

He had been hoping to run into the youngest of the Dillons. If the truth must be told, he had had his eye on those two young

41

girls for years and was only waiting for them to get big enough. He didn't suspect that other men had had similar ambitions and even the affair of the earlier evening did not entirely disperse his hopes that they were still safe for him.

Crossing on to the railway line he was treading down the sleepers when Josie Dillon, who had had three children, came down the slope towards a well. She was smoking a cigarette, which she put out on seeing him. Was the girl afraid of him as of a priest? It looked like it, and he did not want to give that impression of himself, which was, in his opinion, a false impression. Yet the girl might have been right, for on taking a second look at her he knew that he just didn't associate with that class of person. She was the type of woman whom he often saw in the slums of the town of a fair day.

To find out about the sisters he would have to speak to her, so he spoke, much to her surprise, for he had often passed her by before with his head in the air. He only said it was a nice evening, and the girl took it for granted that he meant something else.

'Are you coming down the line?' she inquired.

'Good God! no,' he said. 'I'm late for the Mission as I am.'

He raced up the slope and out of her range as quickly as he could, praying as he ran that nobody saw him. Bad as he was, if he got the name of being seen with one of the Dillons he'd be ruined. Some men could take life easily. Some could dabble in sin, but it didn't fit into his life. He made a promise to the Sacred Heart that if he hadn't been seen he would go to the Mission every single evening, and to Confession on the next Saturday.

When he found out that nobody had seen him – if they had there would be talk – he was somewhat annoyed with himself for making rash promises – but he would keep them.

The little tillage fields and the struggle for existence broke every dramatic fall. A layer of sticky soil lay between the fires in the heart preventing a general conflagration. The Mission had lifted up the limp body of society in Dargan, but as soon as the pressure was relaxed it fell back again and the grass grew over the penitential sod.

With Tarry it was different. He believed that of all the people in the parish he alone took religion seriously. Too seriously, for being too serious meant that it was not integrated in his ordinary life. When the ordinary man went to Confession he rambled on with a list of harmless sins, ignoring all the ones that would have filled Tarry with remorse. When Tarry went to Confession that Saturday night he had the misfortune, contrary to his own well-thought-out arrangements, to mention unusual sins.

The Confessor was the monk he had met on the road.

'What sins do you remember since your last Confession?' the monk asked.

'I read books, father,' Tarry replied before he had time to think. He knew at once that he had made a mistake, for that started the monk off.

'What sort of books?'

Tarry did not want to admit that he only read school books and newspapers and it would appear that he was telling a lie if he didn't try to mention some books. So he said: 'Shaw, father.'

He had read about Shaw in the newspapers, but had never read a line of Shaw's.

'Have you a Rosary?' asked the Confessor.

Tarry had not but he said: 'Yes, father' in the hope of getting out of the confessional as quickly as possible. He had made it awkward enough as it was.

'You should read the *Messenger of the Sacred Heart*,' said the Confessor. 'Do you ever read the little *Messenger*?'

'Yes, father.'

'Continue to read it, my child; in that little book you will find all the finest literature written by the greatest writers. And give up this man, Shaw.'

In all he could not have been less than twenty minutes in the confessional and considering that there was a long impatient queue on both sides of the confessional – among whom were Charlie and Eusebius – and that that confessor had the reputation of being very quick and easy – which was why he had such queues waiting to tell their sins to him, no wonder that Tarry's lengthy period in the confession box caused such surprise.

'Shaw's a hard man,' remarked Charlie later, when they were standing outside Magan's shop. Charlie hadn't the faintest idea who Shaw was but he thought that by mentioning the name someone might reveal the secret behind it. No one knew, and Charlie was disappointed.

'You were a long time in the box with the priest, I hear,' said the mother when he got home. 'Did you kill a man or what? . . . You'll have to cut them yellow weeds in the Low Place the morrow and not have the fields a show to the world. What did you say that made him keep you?'

'It's a sin to tell a thing like that.'

'Whatever you do anyway, I wouldn't like to think of you knocking around Dillon's house, not that I'd ever believe you'd do anything, but you know the big-mouths that's about this place.'

'You needn't worry.'

The Mission came to an end with a brilliant display of lighted candles and the massed congregation of old men and women straightening their bent backs and vowing to renounce the World, the Flesh and the Devil. They promised to control their passions, and Tarry, as he watched the scene of self-abnegation from the gallery, got a queer creepy feeling in the nerves of his face which something that was ludicrous and pathetic always made him feel. Petey Meegan was thumping his breast and looking up towards the coloured window with an ecstatic gaze.

Old thin-faced, long-nosed Jenny Toole had a frightened look, thinking of the dangers she faced in a world of violent men.

The crowds went home and once again the clay hand was clapped across the mouth of Prophecy.

He cut the ragweeds and the thistles the following day. The yellow maggots wearing football jerseys which crept on the blossom fell to the ground. These maggots would become winged if they had lived long enough. Some day he, too, might grow wings and be able to fly away from this clay-stricken place. Ah, clay! It was out of clay that wings were made. He stared down at the dry little canyons in the parched earth and he loved that dry earth which could produce a miracle of wings.

44

He thought of Mary Reilly. By a miracle the day might come when he'd have no trouble in getting her – or one even more beautiful. Greater miracles had happened. He hoped that she did not think that he was really responsible for the mauling she got at Drumnay cross-roads, for he wasn't. Indeed, that was the last thing he would think of doing. It wouldn't be past Eusebius, for all his talk.

He would like to be able to warn the girl of the dangers she was going through, warn her of men like Charlie and some of those other slick blackguards who frequented the dance hall and who were such close friends of Father Markey. Ah, please God she would mind herself. He convinced himself that the curate's brother who sometimes visited Reilly's with the curate was a decent fellow. A rabbit darted from a clump of bushes and he flung a stone at it, forgetting for the moment his pensive thoughts. Looking through the hedge he saw his field of potatoes and turnips and the sight of them doing so well put every other problem out of his mind.

3

Tarry went to the horses' stable for the winkers. Happening to look into the manger he found a fresh-laid egg. He picked up the egg, cracked it on the edge of the old pot in which the mare got her oats and drank it. It was not that he liked raw eggs but he believed that raw eggs produced great virility. Stallions got a dozen raw eggs in a bucket of new milk every day during the season.

Standing in the doorway of the stable he felt good and terribly strong. A man is happy and poetic in health and strength. The stable in summer with the dust of last year's straw on the floor was to Tarry the most romantic place he knew. Sitting in the manger smoking and reading was paradise. But he had work to do now.

Walking through the meadow in summer was a great excitement. The simple, fantastic beauty of ordinary things growing – marsh-marigolds, dandelions, thistles and grass. He did not ask things to have a meaning or to tell a story. To be was the only story.

The sun had come out through the haze and the morning was very warm. The cackle of morning had ceased. The songs of the birds were blotted out by the sun.

Paddy Callan, May's father, was walking diagonally across the hill beside their house looking a little sadly at his rood of turnips which had failed badly. This gave Tarry much satisfaction. His pleasure did not live long for just then he heard the wild neigh of a mare coming down the lane at Cassidy's gate and presently sighted the animal. Eusebius was getting some trade for that stallion of his, though Tarry, wishfully thinking, thought that no sane man would bring a mare to such a miserable beast that wasn't sixteen hands high. Considering that Reilly had a prize stallion, seventeen three in height, at stud less than a mile away this was surprising. Tarry satisfied himself that only bad pays, men with ponies and old mares, would come to Eusebius' stallion. Flynn's mare was in foal by Reilly's sire, although Eusebius had been letting his beast to mares the previous year.

He caught the mare easily enough, for she was lazy at this time, and led her after him to the stable.

The harness wasn't in the best condition. The collar needed lining and the traces were tied with bits of wire in two places. He couldn't find the hames-strap. Searching for it between a rough wooden ceiling and the galvanized roof he found a torn school reader which he usually enjoyed reading while evacuating his bowels in the stable. He put it in his pocket in case he'd take a notion to read in the field.

'Come home for your dinner about half-twelve,' said his mother.

'Right.'

'And don't come till we call you.'

'I'll not come at all if that 'ill satisfy you,' said Tarry peevishly.

'Begod there's a powerful piece of turnips,' Eusebius was saying as he leaned over a low stone fence upon which moss and briars were growing, and which was the march-fence dividing a field of Cassidy's from Flynn's.

'Not so bleddy bad, as the fella said,' Tarry agreed. The field of two and a half acres was one-third taken up with turnips and the rest, with the exception of three drills of cabbages, with potatoes. Tarry looked across at the drills and the goodness of the crop flowed through the heat of his passionate desiring mind like a cool river. He remembered the damp evening on which he sowed them with love. The dry clay too was so beautiful. As they talked, Tarry's mind adventured over and back that rutted headland with its variety of wonders. From where he stood to the cross hedge bordering the grazing field. Every weed and stone and pebble and briar all along that ordinary headland evoked for him the only real world – the world of the imagination. And the rank smell of the weeds!

What is a flower?

Only what it does to a man's spirit is important.

Something happened when Tarry looked at a flower or a stone in a ditch. Sometimes he went with visitors to what were called beauty spots and these fools would point and say: 'Isn't that a wonderful scene?' But these scenes did nothing to him and were not wonderful.

Eusebius had his elbows on a flat stone as he spoke. He had tackle – hobbles and ropes – on his shoulder as he was on his way to castrate young bulls for someone.

'Isn't it a bit late in the season for cutting calves?' Tarry suggested.

'Not at all, the flies didn't start yet.'

Eusebius was a marvellous man for trying to pick up loose money in this way. He was always on the look-out for any game that had ready money in it. He also went in for castrating young pigs but he had the name of not being very lucky so that his trade in this line was rather thin. At the time he was also dabbling in smuggling. Then there was the stallion.

Tarry thought Eusebius a greedy man for the world, and a mean man too in spite of all his gaiety.

'See any women lately?' Eusebius asked.

'None that counted, anyway.'

'Any word about the Reilly one?'

'I think that all blew over. The Mission killed it. All the same it was a damn mean thing of Charlie to give out my name that night. That was a dirty lousy thing to do. I'll get that fella yet or I'll call myself a damn poor class of a man.' Tarry spoke petulantly, as a weak man. Eusebius crossed the fence and accompanied Tarry down the drill.

'I say, there's flaming great spuds. You must have shoved on the potash, no matter what you say.'

'Only the hundred,' said Tarry with an in-drawn breath of self-satisfaction.

'Near closing the alleys. That's fierce for this time of the year.'

'Easy there, Polly. You're not in earnest about that, are you?'

'Only what I hear. All women's as bad as the Dillons if they get the chance.'

These remarks wounded Tarry very deeply. He wanted to

sustain his illusions about human nature. He did not want to believe these things – until, perhaps, he had had his fill of lust.

'I believe that nearly every girl in this place is a virgin,' said he, hopefully. Eusebius laughed loudly. 'Huh, huh, huh. Jabus, you're a very innocent fella. I'd say there wouldn't be more than twenty per cent – if there *is* that.'

The mare stopped on the side of the hill. Tarry stood with his back to the plough and standing between the handles settling his mind for a good long talk on his favourite theme.

'You're a desperate man, Eusebius,' he opened. 'To hear you talking a person would imagine all the women in your country was blackguards. That's the kind of Charlie Trainor. Nobody's out for anything else according to him. After all there's more than that in it.'

'You might be right, right enough.'

'I'm sure I'm right. There's very few women like that when it comes to the whipping of crutches. Remember the night we saw him with the Dillon one?'

'Look!'

'Wonder who the devil is it.'

'Might be the bailiffs coming from Carlin's. They have a betten pad up to them.' The two boys stared across the fields watching the clear in the hedges at the turn of the Drumnay lane, two hundred yards distant.

'They'll be sold out before long,' said Eusebius.

'Indeed they will not, Eusebius; they're not that far gone,' said Tarry, who had a greedy notion in his head that they, the Flynns, might be able to slip in and get the Carlins' place for half-nothing – maybe for fifty pounds. It did not occur to him that Eusebius might have eyesight just as good and maybe better, for seeing through deal boards. It is foolish not to recognize the other fellow as as far-seeing a rogue as yourself.

In the middle of the conversation Eusebius suddenly remembered that he had business on hand; the chance of making a few shillings always crashed like a stone through the window of his romantic mind, and he was off. His father was just the same, all gaiety and jocosity till it came to business and then he changed his mood altogether.

Tarry stood in the shadow of the poplars beside the stream musing on the general moral situation in a day-dreamy way. He could get no perspective on life, for life lay warm, too warm, around him, and too close and nearly suffocating. He was up to his neck in life and could not see it to enjoy it. His whole conscious mind was strained in an effort to drag himself up out of the belly of emotion.

Sometimes he would concentrate, saying to himself: I am alive. Those are potatoes there, and that is a blackthorn's root. Life was like a terrible pain which he was trying to analyse away.

He found a long cigarette butt in the lining of his waistcoat and reflected on the irony of it; for the night before when he hadn't a cigarette he had searched every pocket, including the linings, and could find nothing. Now when he had nearly a full packet he found this great long Player butt.

Tarry, musing, got a feeling that someone was near at hand. He was right; his mother was standing on the height above him in the middle of the plot of turnips surveying the scene after having taken good stock of the turnips and of her son's morning work.

She had approached the field from the other end and had managed to come across the stone fence.

'How do you think they're doing?' she asked.

'The best turnips in your country,' he said; 'they're butting a dread; some of them as thick as your thumb. They're fierce turnips.'

'Don't be always boasting like the Callans. The Callans never had anything that wasn't better than anyone else's. Troth you may thank me that they're so good. Only I was at you, you wouldn't sow them that evening. Was that Eusebius you had with you?'

'He was just passing; I hardly had time to talk to him.'

'Oh, that's the right careful boy that knows how to make a shilling. There was two mares up there this morning to his stal-

50

lion – and you always making little of the animal, not sixteen hands high. It's a terror the trade he's getting for that young stallion.'

'He'll get all the bad pays the first year, don't you know that? A new stallion or bull is like a new shop in that way. Nobody ever made money of a stallion or bull.'

'Oh, that 'ill do you, now. A drunken oul' rake never made money of a stallion, but I'll bet you Eusebius won't be so. Troth they'll all pay him. Lord God of Almighty!' Mrs Flynn reflected as her eyes scanned yellow-weeded fields to the east. 'Them Carlins are the unfortunate people. The whole farm – and that's the good dry farm – all going wild. Yellow weeds like a forest. Oh, that was a bad family that couldn't have luck. The abuse they used to give to their father and mother was total dread. Getting up in the morning, at every hour, if the tay wasn't fresh more would have to be wet. And there was a time when Jemmy was as consaitey a boy as went into Dargan chapel. And all the girls that were after him!

'"I could thatch a house with all the women I could get," says he to me. "Yes, I could thatch a house with all the women I could get."'

The mother had come slowly down the drills while her son was driving the mare towards her. 'You shouldn't drive that unfortunate mare too fast,' she said, for in her presence the son had put on a great spurt.

He pulled up. The mother began to speak in a confidential whisper. 'Had Eusebius any news?'

Tarry thought that perhaps his mother had been listening to their talk about girls and was a bit embarrassed. 'Curse o' God on the ha'porth.'

'Aw-haw, catch that fellow to tell you anything! They tell me the grippers were up at Carlins' again. As I said, as bad as they are I was glad the oul' cow, the only four-footed animal they have about the place, wasn't taken. They drove her into Cassidy's field. They'll be out of that before you're much older. They'll be on the broad road as sure, as sure, as sure. And mind you, that's as dry and as warm a farm of land as there is in the parish.

There's a couple of fields there and do you know what it is you could plough them with a pair of asses, they're that free. It's a terrible pity you wouldn't take a better interest in your work and you could be the independentest man in Ireland. You could tell all the beggars to kiss your arse. This rhyming is all right but I don't see anything in it. Sure if I thought there was anything in it I'd be the last person to say a word against it, but – Stand over here!'

Tarry stood facing the point his mother drew attention to.

'Who would that be?' the mother whispered.

They were watching someone, a man, coming at a stoop on the far side of a high hedge beyond Brady's field. He had something on his back.

'Do you know,' said the mother, 'just for cure-ossity you should slip down to the corner and see who the devil's father it is. I'll keep an eye on Polly.'

Tarry crossed the drills quickly and pulling a rotten bush out of a gap in the hedge went into the grazing field.

The man with the sleeper on his back was going at a stoop on the far side of the other hedge that divided Finnegan's Big Hill from Flynn's farm. It was Eusebius.

While he was developing a strong jealousy towards Eusebius who was making such a practice of stealing sleepers that they'd all be caught in the end he saw another man coming at a murderous gallop down Brady's narrow garden. This man was not a railwayman but a small farmer from the opposite side of the railway. No normal observer of the scene would need to be told what it was all about.

Eusebius sized up the situation for he now was shoving the sleeper through a hole in the hedge into Flynn's field.

Having pushed the sleeper through he saw Tarry and, never at a loss, stood his ground until Tarry came up. Then seeing the angry man approaching he climbed through the hole made by the sleeper into Flynn's field.

'Larry Finnegan, he's mad,' Eusebius panted with a laugh that was much strained. Tarry listened.

'He had the sleeper ready to take away, had it over the paling and was going back for another – the greedy dog – when I snaffled it on him. Just for a cod, you know.'

By now the angry Larry had come up but instead of turning on Eusebius he went past without a word with an injured expression.

They hid the sleeper in some briars and Eusebius went back the way he had come.

'Well?' asked the mother when the son returned.

He told her the story.

'There's no luck in a thing like that,' she said. 'If I wanted a thing I'd pay for it and not have people throwing it in your face. Yes, aye,' she said about nothing at all. 'That mare won't take long; you'd want to keep an eye on her. Oh, an unfortunate pack of poor devils. Do you know what?' she declared suddenly on a new and enthusiastic note, 'I think I'll dodge up round Carlins' one of these evenings to see what kind of a place they have at all. I don't know the day or hour I was up there. Since the Mission, they don't get up till evening I hear. When a party quits going to Mass it's a bad sign.'

Tarry saw the possibilities in that move, but not all the possibilities his mother saw.

He had already another small problem in his mind – how to slip off with that sleeper before Eusebius returned for it. He knew what he would do. He would simply change the hiding place and if Eusebius found it well and good – well and good.

Tarry shook the clay out of the heel of his boot and pulled his sock, which had been creeping towards his toes till the heel part was half-way up, tightly on his shin.

He watched his mother as she walked along the bottom headland, slowly sauntering along it sideways looking up the drills with all the contentment that a good crop in a bad season can give to a tiller of the soil.

'There's a drill there,' she shouted, 'and what the devil happened it? You mustn't have put any dung on it.'

She did not expect an answer, and did not wait for one, but opened the wooden gate that led into the field where the cows were. The gate dragged and Tarry could sense her silent criticism as she pulled it open and shut.

About this time Molly was in the habit of coming to the well, and as Tarry had not given up hopes of seducing her in reality as successfully as he did so often in his daydreams he was hoping that his mother would not delay too long with the cows.

A ploughman runs a risk when he daydreams in a stony field – unless his horses are extremely slow-moving and cautious.

The mare seemed to know every turn and twist of her master's mind; instinctively, like a woman. When she stepped over a hidden rock she went still slower. Sometimes she twisted her head round to have a good look at the driver, and sometimes she seemed to be laughing at him.

His mother wandered slowly through the grazing field, musing on the grass.

Tarry settled himself down to enjoy moulding the potatoes. So interested did he get in his work that he didn't 'loose out' till one o'clock. He threw the harness on top of the plough and let the mare eat around the headland.

How pleased his mother was that he hadn't come home before the dinner was ready as he usually did, 'coming in roaring for his dinner like a lion', as his mother expressed it.

He returned to work in an hour, very satisfied, luxuriating in the big feed of potatoes, cabbage and bacon which he had eaten.

He left word with Bridie not to forget to get the paper off the breadman when she went for the bread. Going to look for the sleeper he found it missing, and this vexed him plenty.

Thus was life, and a sensitive man bogged in it.

The nettles, thistles and docks bloomed wildly at the backs of ditches. Life was very rich.

A spirit still buried in the womb of emotion, Tarry hardly ever had experiences that could be named. But one evening shortly afterwards a young heifer had to be brought to the bull, and on that evening he came into contact with something that almost awakened him.

His mother and sisters helped him with the heifer to the gate.

They had intended bringing her to Kerley's bull, the fee for which was only a half-crown, but when the heifer got out the yard gate she dashed up the Drumnay lane, and it's a principle with the people to let a young beast go the way she chooses in a matter of this description. His mother handed him the five shillings which was the service fee for Reilly's bull, a prize short-horn, and Tarry was considering if he'd be able to slip back when his mother and sisters were gone into the house and ring her to Kerley's bull and save a half-crown for himself. He had done that once before and saved not only a half-crown but the whole five bob, for he got the cow bulled by a young unlicensed bull that was grazing in McArdle's field. He had encouraged his mother that a calf out of the famous double-dairy shorthorn that Reilly's had at that time would be a real wonder, and when the calf grew up his mother was never done praising it. The only trouble in a case like this was that the cow mightn't keep the bull the first time, and then you'd have to go back and would have the money spent. So he let the heifer go as she was inclined. She galloped up the road. He had a mind to go back for the bicycle, but changed his mind and slowly followed the heifer. He wondered if he would see Mary and he also hoped that the father had not been a joke and a jeer about his mother's remarks in the market the previous week.

Callan's gate was open but luckily enough she did not see it. The heifer went out of sight round the turn where the hedge was high and overhung the lane. A slight shower had fallen making the dust of the road like velvet. His business seldom took him up this way, so that this evening's walk was for him a mystical adventure.

Places which he had not seen for a week seemed so mysterious, like places in a fantastic foreign land.

As he passed Callan's back lane he looked up towards the house where the trees were dark with greenery. He could see Mrs Callan standing on top of a pit of rotten mangolds staring into the distances of the southern townland. The father's whistle which never became an air – he had no ear for music, nor one belonging to him for that matter – could be heard from the region of the dunghill behind the wooden sheds. May was not visible.

He hurried to catch up with the heifer and found when he went round the next turn that she had strayed into Cassidy's haggard and was nibbling in her wild way at some wizened old potatoes that lay against the wall of the boiler house. Mat Ward, the half-wit (an iron fool really), who worked off and on for Eusebius was squaring a dunghill in the yard; it was strange how Eusebius and his father could always get these loose-idiots to work for them for jaw-wages.

'Will you give us a hand with this heifer?' said Tarry.

Mat laid down the graip with an air of profound wisdom and came slowly towards Tarry and the heifer.

'Nice wee stuff ye have,' said he. 'A bit rough o' the head all the same.'

'She'll have to be doing, Mat,' said Tarry, anxious to get the beast away from the dangerous potatoes which could easily choke a cow beast.

'She'll take no hurt,' said Mat.

They drove the nervous animal on to the road again; Mat's knowing scrutiny as he tried to get a line on the heifer from behind, amused Tarry very much.

'She has the makings of a good bag,' he said, 'a bit shy in the left back quarter, but the makings of a good bag all the same.'

Mat helped Tarry with the heifer round the next turn. Then he stood rubbing the seat of his trousers as he stared after them. There were no gates or gaps on the next stretch of road – until he would be passing Toole's house. He was able to relax and nibble at the leaves of whitethorn as he went along. He wondered if he would see Mary Reilly. He did not wonder too much for she was far beyond his dreams. A man cannot love the impossible.

On either side of him were the little fields. Three fields across was Carlin's half-derelict house. The thatched part of the dwelling was down. The three brothers and two sisters lived in the small slated part. Queer.

A woman was coming down the grass-grown path from Carlins', and Tarry hung on to see who it might be. The gap onto the main Drumnay lane was at this point, so she'd have to pass him. The woman was Eusebius' mother, a very fresh woman for her years and light on her feet. She had a sharp tongue, Tarry knew.

'You'll soon have a free house down there,' she said right out for a start as if she had been thinking about the matter for some time previously.

'How?' asked Tarry, stupidly.

'I hear that Mary is getting a man. If one goes they'll all go.'

'*I* never heard a word about it,' said Tarry, truthfully.

'Oh, and a good man, too.' Changing the subject with that suddenness which one finds among people with something on their minds, she said: 'I was just over at Carlins' with a wee can of milk – their cow is dry – and do you know what I'm going to tell you, they're a proud family. I left her a wee can of cow's milk on the wall beside the garden every morning and evening, and when I come back for me empty can there it is – full of goat's milk. Poor Maggie is up there, and to listen to her you'd swear that they didn't owe anyone a penny. Nothing for her but talk of ladies and gentlemen. One of my girls is coming on her holidays next month, Tarry, and do you know, the last time she wrote she said not to forget to tell you that she was asking for you.'

Tarry suspected nothing.

But he knew why Mrs Cassidy was being so considerate for the Carlins. They were manoeuvring for an opening. Already they had got to store – by the way – several articles of value which the Carlins wanted to put out of the way of the bailiffs. A good Ransome mowing machine that Tarry could have been doing with, and the best iron land roller in the country. And never during saecula would these articles be given back. Oh, never.

Tarry passed Jenny Toole's whitewashed house and skirted the waste land which was the tail-end of what was once a big estate, 'Whitestone Park'. At the moment there was some agitation to have the lands divided up among the small farmers, but as Tarry did not expect to be given any of this land he was inclined to frown on such greed.

Now he had arrived at the entrance to Reilly's farm. The heifer turned in the entrance without any trouble.

Tarry rubbed his face and cursed himself for not shaving, in case he met Mary. The patch on the knee of his trousers also disturbed his self-confidence. If he had only put on his good trousers! He took off his cap and ran his fingers through his hair. He softened the stare of his eyes so as to look more gentle and poetical. Mary had been going to the convent and Tarry knew that convents taught girls to appreciate the poetic things. He giggled to himself thinking on the foolishness of nuns. Poetry is the most lustful and egotistical of spirits.

Young Paddy Reilly saw the heifer coming and had the gate open. From some unseen place beyond the haggard the low, awful roar of the bull could be heard. Then he appeared profound and massive, pawing the earth in the corner of the big field beside the haggard.

The Reillys were not aristocrats. The father was a small farmer's son who by hard work and the capacity for making others work for him had graduated into the ranks of the semi-gentleman farmers. His farm ran to the Louth border and partook of some of the qualities of a Louth farm – big fields, big horses, big carts.

Returning with his heifer, Tarry felt very disappointed at not having seen Mary Reilly.

He was trying to sneak up close to the heifer to give her a smart blow of the ash plant on the spine – to take the hump off her back – when who should appear coming slowly around the bend only Mary. She was dressed in a light blue cotton dress and her long black hair hung loose over her shoulders. He had seen this girl many times before, but this was the first time she was revealed to him. Like the average tiller of the soil he could not see men and women in terms of sex. A mare was as big and strong as a horse, a cow was, in her way, as impressive as a bull. Women and men were just people living, not sexes.

Tarry had never observed the sexual differences between men and women until this moment. Mary Reilly was tall, and if as Tarry's mother had said she had a large bottom, Tarry suddenly realized now that this part of her was different from the bottoms of the ordinary country girls. All the girls, with the exception of May Callan, were squat, and as the country phrase had it – 'duck-arsed'. They were made for work, for breeding, their centre of gravity was low. But here was someone who was made for joy, a breaker of hearts.

Tarry's mind was paralysed by the sight of her. He tried hurriedly to think of something appropriate to say, but decided in the end that the best thing to do would be completely to ignore her until such time as he had some sort of plan. So when they met and she moved up on the bank to let the heifer pass, he gave all his attention to the heifer to avoid having to make a decision, and so he only guessed that she smiled and said, 'Hello, Tarry.'

She was only about nineteen, nearly ten years younger than he was, but she carried within her what Tarry knew was a terrible power of which she was as yet unconscious.

He didn't recover himself till he was passing Toole's house, and then he had begun to daydream all the fine things he had said to her and she to him. So excited was he that he was now thinking his thoughts aloud. Being accosted by Jenny Toole, who came to the entrance to her street and was leaning on a graip watching him approach, he quietly changed his talk into a song.

'You were at Reilly's bull,' she said. 'Ah, indeed, nothing for some people only the rich.'

Jemmy Kerley was her first cousin.

'That's right,' said Tarry with the suggestion of a sneer. He did not like Jenny Toole, a bitter old maid, and she was one of the few people of whose evil power he was afraid.

Although he was fairly scientific-minded he harboured old superstitions that a bad wish from someone like that could do him – or the heifer – no good. He knew that was all nonsense, but just to be on the safe side – the answer if it did no good could do no harm – he said quietly to himself, directing the remark back at the woman – 'God bless your eyes and your heart', which was the traditional remark in cases of this kind.

The summer sun was going down in a most wonderful yellow ball behind the hills of Drumnay. It turned the dirty upstairs windows of Cassidy's house into stained glass.

O the rich beauty of the weeds in the ditches, Tarry's heart cried. The lush nettles and docks and the tufts of grass. Life pouring out in uncritical abundance.

Tarry was lifted above himself now in a purer kind of dream. He concentrated on observing, on contemplating, to clean his soul. He enumerated the different things he saw: Kerley's four cows looking over a hedge near a distant house waiting to be milked. A flock of white geese in the meadow beside Cassidy's bog. He heard the rattle of tin cans being picked up from the stones outside a door – somebody going to the well for water. But what bird was making that noise like the ratchet of a new free-wheel? He stared through the bushes where the blue forget-me-nots and violets were creeping. No bird was there.

He hurried after the heifer. Passing Cassidy's house Tarry was suddenly proud of the heifer, and it occurred to him now as it often occurred before how nice and idealistic looking, how gentle-eyed and good-natured were the cattle he reared compared to the wicked-looking ugly beasts Eusebius reared. There was something in it, he imagined.

Mrs Flynn was leaning over the low wall by the gate enjoying the peace of a lovely summer evening when Tarry appeared in sight. She was waiting to have conversations with passers-by.

She rushed to open the gate, saying as they drove the heifer in: 'Had you much trouble with her?'

'Plenty,' said Tarry, to gain sympathy.

'We'd better put her in for the night and not have the other cows lepping on her. Mary, give us a hand.'

Mary, who was shutting in the sow, grabbed a yard brush and turned the heifer towards the stable door.

'Well, that's that,' said the mother. 'I hope she keeps.'

Aggie and Bridie were dressed for the road, waiting in the kitchen for May to give them the call.

Tarry tested the tyres of his bicycle which stood outside the cart-house door. His mother followed him and began to speak very confidentially: 'Petey Meegan sent word the day.'

'About what?' said Tarry.

'He has a notion of Mary. But don't breathe this to the face of clay. The Missioners must have shook him up.'

Tarry was a little astonished. 'He's a bit past himself,' he said.

'Arra, nonsense. He's a good, sober, industrious boy with a damn good farm of land in Miskin. And an empty house. Oh, girls can't be too stiff these days. They're all hard pleased and easy fitted.'

'But he must be well over the fifty mark,' whispered Tarry devoutly.

'That's young enough for a healthy man. And mind you, Mary is no chicken. Only the day I was thinking that she's within a kick of the arse of thirty. Troth if she gets him she'll be lucky. The other two are often enough on the road, and the devil the big rush is on them. As Charlie Trainor says, they're like horse-dung, you never walk the road but you meet them. I always say to these here, marry the first man that asks you. There's only three classes of men a woman should never marry – a delicate man, a drunken man, and a lazy man. I'm not so sure that the lazy man isn't the worst. Are you goin' away this evening, too?'

'Had a mind to go down as far as the New Road.'

'Surely to God you wouldn't marry a thing like that,' said May Callan to Mary Flynn as the two girls gossiped, with the hedge between them, at the bottom of Callan's hill where May had come to milk the cows. 'How could you bring yourself to go to bed with a hairy oul' fellow like Petey?'

Tarry, who was scouring out a bog-hole at the bottom of the garden, from which water could be drawn during the drought, rested on the shaft of his shovel to listen in.

'That could be got over,' said Mary, a little pensively.

'Well, my mother says you must be a shocking fool,' said May. 'After all, you're not that hard up for a man.'

'I don't know,' Mary sighed.

Tarry pulled a wisp of grass and ran it down the shovel shaft to wipe off the mud. This movement must have made the girls aware of his listening presence, for May hunkered by the side of a cow and the sing-sing-sing of milk going into an empty tin can echoed in the evening hollows like a new bird's song.

'Might see you later,' said Mary, who was nibbling at the leaves of the bushes, very worried.

'I'm not so sure, for my mother is going out,' said May.

Mary Flynn wandered towards the house and presently was in conversation with Bridie who was cleaning the hen house.

'You were talking to gabby-guts,' said Bridie. 'What had *she* to say?'

'Oh, nothing.'

Tarry came up from the bog-hole and stood the shovel by the hen house in case Bridie should want it. 'Who's inside?' he asked.

Tarry found himself staring half-vacantly at his sisters.

Between the three Flynn girls there was little to choose. They were all the same height, around five feet two – low-set, with dull clayey faces, each of them like a bag of chaff tied in the middle with a rope – breasts and buttocks that flapped in the wind. When they were unwashed and undressed in the morning a stranger passing seeing them would hardly be able to say who was who. They were all the daughters Mrs Flynn ever had. They had not advanced with the times sufficiently to change from the old notion of staying about the home until some man came looking for them. Most of the other neighbours' daughters had gone off, lots of them to be nurses in England, or to become shop girls in local towns or factory workers in the newly established rope-factory in Shercock, but the Flynns had a great desire to be farmers' wives.

Tarry saw them at the closest range, but he was too close to observe them as anything but sisters.

Mary, who was the eldest of the family, twenty-nine and a year and seven months older than her brother, was the most un-attractive of the three. She seemed to be continuously wearing a pout like one with a grievance, yet for all that she was the one most likely to get a husband. Some women who are beautiful bring out a falseness in men, set up complexities which are unfavourable to marriage combines in the tillage country. A man

62

meeting Mary Flynn would be his own natural self – except in the case of such a tragic person as Petey Meegan. And *he* had made overtures to Mary which proved to Tarry what he had often considered, that the attraction of the possible is in the end more powerful than that of the unattainable.

It was within the bounds of possibility that all the sisters would eventually get husbands of some sort. In that lay another worry of Tarry's – The crookedest, oldest, poorest small farmer would be looking for money with a wife; and where in the case of his sisters was even one hundred pounds a piece to come from? He had often mentioned these worries to his mother, and she had always replied: 'Let them produce the man first and then it 'ill be time enough to talk about money.'

He knew that his mother had a few pounds in the bank all right, but as far as he could make out it couldn't amount to more than a single hundred at the very outside. He would like to know how much money she really had in the bank. He did remember one day being in the bank with her when a man who had been paid by cheque for cattle wanted to cash it. The bank manager signified that Mrs Flynn's name on the back of the cheque would do, but she pretended that she couldn't write her name.

It was on the strength of these few pounds that his sisters were depending, and Tarry did not like it. They should go and try to make a living elsewhere, but when he thought of them sympathetically, where could they go unless to England to be nurses? They were too proud to do that. So there wasn't much chance of Tarry having a clear house into which to bring a wife. Yet, except when he wanted to make excuses for himself, he admitted in his heart that even if the house were empty he would hardly marry any girl in that country who would be willing to endure the life he could give her.

The ugliness of his sisters was a puzzle to Tarry. How did they come to be so indifferent-looking while he was well above the average of men in the place? The mother said it was from a grandfather on the father's side – 'a man that you'd think was reared in a pot,' she said.

For all their seeming likeness to each other in externals they were quite individual. When Tarry forgot himself sufficiently to let his natural sympathy flow, he saw them as three souls as new and wonderful as individual souls always are.

They surely had their dreams, too. Beneath the conventional cliché which they wore as a defence the bleeding reality of intense life poured its red-hot stream of feeling.

Aggie was the most religious-minded, but all of them had strong faith. In the struggle it was hard contemplating the luxurious ecstasy of God in the fields or on the Altar. Yet they did. Their real devoutness, though they did not know it, was in their faith in life.

Bridie, the youngest, was only twenty-one. She had a wild temper and a sharp tongue. She was mean to her brother on many occasions, and did not fail to make a show of him in front of a crowd on a couple of occasions by charging him with stealing her money which she had been hiding in a flower pot deep down in the clay.

Except on very rare occasions Tarry realized that he did not care for his sisters, and was not worried how they fared in life. His own problems were too pressing.

While the girls were talking and Tarry was thinking, the heavy footsteps, which there was no mistaking, of Petey Meegan could be heard approaching Flynn's gate. He coughed his usual short cough to announce his approach.

Before he had arrived at the yard gate Mary was in the middle of a savagely belittling speech about him – 'the dirty oul', crooked oul' eejut. It's saying his prayers he ought to be.'

Tarry was depressed on hearing her opinion of a possible husband. If she didn't accept him – and by all appearances she would not – there was very little chance of his ever having a free house to bring a woman into.

Not to make the poor old fellow's welcome seem too freezing, Tarry went towards the gate to say a few words of comfort. As he went he could hear his sister's repeated – 'oul' eejut, oul' eejut, oul' eejut' from the door of the hen house. How pitiful it was to hear an oldish man trying to be young in his talk and actions.

Coming up to the gate he sprightlied up his plough-crookened step and tried to straighten his humped shoulders. He looked any age between fifty and the age of an old oak. He was wearing his Sunday trousers, and this made still more obvious the man's ancient position.

When he opened up the discussion on a frivolous topic – the previous Sunday night's dance – Tarry's embarrassment turned to sorrow for the man. Tarry switched the conversation to what he believed were more appropriate subjects by asking him how his turnips were doing.

'Who cares about turnips in weather like this?' said he.

'I gave a second moulding to my spuds, Petey,' said Tarry, struggling to swing the discussion.

But nothing could stop Petey from wanting to discuss light romance. The sow trailed through the yard and Tarry pretended to be driving her somewhere, but the man never noticed the animal at all.

In the end there was nothing Tarry could do but invite the man into the house. They sat by the half-dead fire alone for half an hour. The two sisters had slipped in and up the stairs without coming into contact with Petey. The upstairs floor creaked and Petey listened uneasily.

This was one of the most awkward situations Tarry had ever to deal with, and he wished his mother would soon return.

In the end the talk lagged.

'Well, that's the way,' said Petey, which was the phrase he used to smother a sigh.

And Tarry replied, 'That's the way.'

Petey took out a packet of cigarettes, though he was a pipe smoker, and a tobacco chewer.

'You're getting swanky,' remarked Tarry, in an attempt to break the deadness.

'Yes, that's the way,' sighed Petey on a different note.

'That's the way,' sighed Tarry back. He got up and put water in the kettle.

'Where the devil's these women of ours?' he said, partly to himself. Petey did not answer. He was sitting with his head between his legs smoking the cigarette in amateurish fashion, one half of it wet in his mouth, while he stared at the tongs.

He rubbed his fingers along the bricks of the arch, and eventually forced himself to gulp: 'The man that built that arch knew his job.'

'The Ring Finnegan,' said Tarry.

'He was the right smoke doctor,' said Petey, but without much enthusiasm.

Tarry hung on the kettle and blew up the fire. Then he went to the door to listen for his mother's homecoming. Not a sign of her. If Aggie was here atself. The only sound he could hear was the soft laughter of his two sisters and May as they went giggling down towards the main road. He was properly in the lurch now.

God, how he wished his mother would come home and take a great burden off his hands. It wasn't merely the boredom of having to keep a depressed man company, but he wanted to take a quick walk round by Drumnay cross-roads on the off chance of catching a sight of Mary Reilly.

He was worried about that girl as he never had been worried about any of the other neighbours' girls. His mind overflowed her like a warm tide. He became jittery. He knew from experience that when he wanted anything, like this wanting to wander round by the cross-roads, he would have to wear out his patience. He knew that a man never got anything – while he desperately wanted it. To himself he said a quiet prayer: 'Jesus, Mary and Joseph, keep Mary Reilly for me.'

'I suppose I'm as well be on the move,' said Petey, rising and stretching himself as if he were bored with it all. 'As the man said, I have a few things to do, and, like that, I better go before night falls.'

'Aw, take your time: I have the kettle near boiling.'

'No, I'm better be going.'

At the doorway he turned: 'I suppose,' he said very casually, 'these women of yours won't be home for a while?'

'My mother ought to be home anyway, Petey, and you're as well wait.'

'No, sure I can come some other evening.'

And he went.

No sooner had he departed than Mrs Flynn arrived. 'What have you the kettle on for?' she asked.

Tarry told her the whole story.

'The devil thrapple her anyway,' she said. She hung the umbrella, which she had used as a walking stick, on the side of the wall and hurried about the house. 'You may as well make a sup now when you have the kettle boiled . . . Oh, no, I wouldn't much mind Mary saying things like that. That doesn't count. If I had to be here I'd tell her something. Yes, hard pleased and easy fitted, that's what she is. Oh, I saw ones like her before and they'd want a man made for them. Ah-ha, I saw them after and they weren't so stiff. Oh, wait till she comes home.'

'All the same she'll hardly take him,' said Tarry, resignedly.

'Be my safe sowl she will,' said the mother with determination. 'She's not going to lie up on me here and a man coming looking for her . . . The tay is in the wee canister beside the soda . . . Be me safe sowl she'll marry him or take the broad road and her health. Wouldn't go to be a nurse in England like the Cassidy girls. If she couldn't be trained in Vincent's in Dublin she wouldn't be a nurse at all. Wanted me to plank down a darling seventy pounds to get her trained in Dublin – the tinker! Where would I get seventy pounds? . . . You made this tay too strong. We won't be able to sleep after this.

'Do you know what, I'm just after coming down from Carlins and there's not a blessed thing about the place that Eusebius hasn't whipped over to his place – the roller that you were always saying you could get and the good reaping mill. Still, if you'd be said by, I have a little plan of me own and if all goes well we might do better than so.'

'Will they be able to pay the debts?' Tarry asked.

'Oh, never, never, never. Sure they're there and not the slightest bit of worry on them no more than if they were as rich as John Magan. I was putting it on to her about selling the cow – she's as good a cow on her third calf as there is in the country – and I might as well be talking to the wall. They laughed at me.'

Tarry wished his mother would not be so mysterious about her plans. If she took him into her confidence she might find that he was as cute a businessman as anyone else. But she would tell him nothing. She was treating him as an irresponsible person and that wasn't good for him.

'You're not going out at this hour of the evening, Tarry?'

'I'll not bother me head,' said Tarry. He knew it was too late. He was easy. Mary Reilly would be home by now. He walked through the yard full of a great loneliness. Everybody was happier than he. The quiet night falling and the Evening Star and the young Moon and the sighing fields made him feel a queer sadness. There was something in him different from other men and women. He always did the peculiar thing, one peculiar thing which yet he could not define, which spoiled his chances of happiness.

In his self-pity he said to himself: I have to carry a cross. He did not want to carry a cross. He wanted to be ordinary. But the more he tried to shake the burden free the more weighty did it become and the more it stuck to his shoulders. His mother came out to the corner of the yard, listened for a while at the horses' stable door, then took the poe which had been an-airing in the fork of a bush beside the dung-hill and returned to the house. The bats flew over Tarry's head. From the main road came the loud laughter of boys and girls.

'Do you hear Bridie?' said the mother from the doorway. 'She'll be heard where she won't be seen.'

While the mother was getting ready to say her prayers Tarry took a candle and went upstairs to a corner of his bedroom and sitting on the edge of the bed took a writing-pad and began to write verses. Yards and yards of despair he wrote about his love for Mary Reilly.

> O God above
> Must I forever live in dreams of love?
> Must I forever see as in a glass
> The loveliness of life before me pass?

The table at which he sometimes wrote was the remains of an old sewing machine, covered with dust and grease and candle-grease. The room was a typical country bedroom, its walls covered with holy pictures. Reading about artistic things Tarry had once suggested to his mother that they should take down all those ugly pictures. She thought him the most atrocious black-guard: 'Is it them splendid pictures? Why there's three pictures there and the likes of them is not in the parish. I bought them second-hand and gave fifteen shillings apiece for them in Mick Duffy's last Easter was eight years. Troth and sowl they'll not be shifted while I'm here.' She didn't stop at that but drove the matter home: 'The pictures you do be talking about are like the bottle of wine. Yes, talking about giving five pounds for a bottle of wine.'

Tarry often regretted ever having mentioned the pictures or the bottle of wine. He had only read that there were rare wines which were sold at very high rates, and mentioned the matter to his mother. She threw it in his face at every opportunity.

The ghosts of night came in the uncurtained windows, and Tarry grew a little afraid. Afraid of his father's ghost. It was in this room his father died less than five years ago.

While his father lived he often told him that he'd never be afraid, but his father said that we would be afraid to see our nearest and dearest. The flickering candle added to his nervousness. His mother starting her evening prayers might have added something more eerie still to the atmosphere – but it was a human voice near.

He couldn't think while she prayed:

'Holy Mary, Mother of God, pray for us ... cat, down out of that and don't be trying to lift the lid of that can ... sinners now and at the hour of our ... Tarry, come down out of that ... death, Amen.'

4

For several days and even weeks the mother was able to see some good in books and dreaming. Wasn't it Tarry's romantic talk with Petey Meegan which had excited that man to want to make a liaison with the Flynns? For all that she was sometimes dim to the sense of it all and said so.

'I can't see anything in it at all. What does it mean?'

'What does anything mean?' was his answer. 'What does Drumnay and Miskin and Dargan and the work day after day and year after year mean? Does that ever occur to you? Are any of these people going anywhere except to the grave?' For a moment he laid bare the myth of living and was filled with remorse for his sin. That was a real sin – to tear up the faith and show nothing but futility.

He did not need to have been so troubled, for Life defending the wound of Reality flowed over it, and the warm blood was no longer exposed to the harsh light.

The mother's depression soon lifted and she was being swept along in the shouting, forgetful throng of people.

'If this Mary one goes they may all go,' she said as she moved the curtain aside to look towards the main road.

'It's a fact,' said Tarry contentedly. He was kneeling by the fire heating a piece of iron.

'Bedad, there's someone coming in from the Big Road,' said the mother, 'it's ... come here you that has the good eyesight. It's the process-server going up to Carlin's. Where's me clean apron till I go out and talk to him.'

It was the process-server all right.

He was a very friendly fellow, on terms of good will with all the people in the districts through which he operated. He was never averse to letting anyone read through his bunch of civil bills and summonses. Now he was running his thumb through the pink documents like a bank man counting pound notes while Tarry and his mother listened with their mouths open.

'There's one for Joe Connolly of Lisdrum and here's another for Jack Hamill, and . . .'

'Musha, what's the matter with Joe Connolly?' asked the mother. 'Sure, he's one of the best-off men in the county. I saw him in the market last Wednesday week.' The process-server was running through the documents for the most interesting ones . . . 'I had one here somewhere . . . Joe is in trouble over a girl. The father is suing him for seduction.'

'Ah, you're a liar, Tommy! That man's sixty if he's a day, and he has a family of grown boys and girls of his own. I wouldn't even it to him.'

'There you are now, ma'am; it's hard to be up to the men that's going these days. I had one here and whatever the damn devil happened to it. Ah, here she is. Have a look at that one.'

'For Father Daly!' said the woman in amazement. 'That bates the little dish. That's a terror. Fifty pound in debt! The parish priest! Who'd think that?'

'He'll not let it go to Court . . . Good evening, Eusebius,' said the process-server. While they were talking Eusebius dashed up the road on his bicycle without a word.

'What hurry can be on him?' said the mother.

'I saw a mare going up to the stallion,' explained Tarry.

'It's late in the season for a mare to be going up,' said the mother.

'I better hurry after him,' said the process-server, throwing his leg over his bicycle.

'To Carlin's you're going, I suppose?' said the mother.

'I have three bills for them the day – one for Tom and two for Jemmy – and sure, like that, I have orders to seize for the past five years. I don't like to lift the cow. This Eusebius up here is grazing the ground but you'd never catch a beast of his on the ground, though I could have taken a pair of bullocks once. And would you believe me, Mrs Flynn, he never as much as said thank you. No, a mean man.'

'Mean is no name for him, Tommy,' said the mother. 'Would

you say would any greedy devil buy the place on the quiet, Tommy?'

Tommy thought that it was quite possible. He heard that a couple of offers had been made for the farm, but he couldn't be sure.

'Wouldn't they ait you for land round here?' said the mother.

'Ait is right,' said the process-server.

'What do you think of that?' said she to her son, when the process-server was gone.

'He lives high,' said he, thinking she was referring to the parish priest.

'Ah, you're the slackest man I ever met. You couldn't see that Eusebius was bursting himself to clear his cattle off Carlin's when he heard the process-server was coming.'

She walked through the street musing: 'Some fine day some cute boyo will slip in and buy that place of Carlin's over all our heads. Oh, as sure as sure can be. Take the cans and go to the well for water. Yes, as sure as sure as sure.'

For a while that problem took a rest and the other one of Petey Meegan's proposed alliance with the family cropped up. Petey came down later in the evening and left two baskets of dirty eggs to be collected at Flynn's by the higgler whose van passed that way every Tuesday evening. It was a good excuse.

Tarry was forced to stay in to keep the old fellow company and to drug his mind with learned talk. The daughters invariably disappeared on Petey's arrival, which was rather unsatisfactory.

There seemed to Tarry to be something unhealthy in the visitor's surrender to the drone of conversation. For all Petey's crude appearance there was a feminine quality in him which in its yielding way was having a very deleterious effect on Tarry's mind.

He mentioned the matter to his mother and she laughed. 'You want to get away, that's all. What could be queer about him?'

Tarry didn't know. 'But why doesn't Mary stay in an odd time atself?'

'Troth, she'll have to in future,' said the mother.

72

The next evening Petey surprised Mary in the house and began to joke with her. She was cruel.

'Ha,' said he, 'I hear you have a fella from the town these days.'

'Shut up, you jack, you,' said Mary.

Petey smiled faintly and Tarry knew that he was adjudging that the girl's abuse was a good sign.

'Can't you be dacent for once?' said the mother. 'And another thing, don't be always going down the road or yous 'ill get a bad name. Petey, you mustn't mind these young ones, they have no sense. How is your turnips doing?'

Like this they talked. Mary left and Petey tried to accompany her to the gate, but she left him standing with his mouth half open, speechless.

The mother made tea for the suitor which he drank with even a louder smack than was usual on the Drumnay side of the hills.

That fared very well. No business was transacted that evening and it did not seem that any business would ever be transacted. But the next evening didn't the brave Petey arrive, accompanied by one of the McArdles and with the old-fashioned bottle of whiskey in his pocket.

On the first sight of them Mary whipped out the gate and away down the road. This didn't deter the spokesman, who began to sing the praises of Petey. Tarry remembered with traces of laughter some of the speech:

'Here is none of your fly-the-kites, Mrs Flynn. He could go where there's more money but he's not looking for money. Good men aren't got on the tops of the bushes these days. He has fourteen acres of what-you-might-call good land – with a drink in every field. He doesn't owe a penny piece to any man. He only lives across the hill and if ever you wanted a turn done you wouldn't be stuck.'

He said a lot more in a sing-song voice as though he had learned it off by heart. The mother agreed that he was as good a take as any girl could want 'in these bad times'.

'Or in any times,' said the spokesman.

'Whatever *you* say. But what's the use of talking. Can I make her marry the man?'

Next thing the spokesman delivered his piece belittling the girl, which was a traditional part of the argument. 'It won't stop her growing,' said he. 'Mind, I'm not saying she's ould, but it's time she was getting a man. I don't want to make little of any woman's daughter, but amn't I saying what's right? What are you going to do about it?'

'What *can* I do about it?'

'Surely you can drive in the heifer?' said he.

'Like oul' hell I can drive her in,' said the mother.

Petey kept his mouth – in the words of the mother, 'as tight shut as a crow's arse,' throughout this discussion. There he sat as pleased as could be, imagining that he was deeply involved in life. This would be something to talk about – the time he went looking for the wife in Flynn's. The mother took a doubtful view of the man's sincerity and agreed with Tarry that there was something unnatural about the man.

Having extracted some food for his ego from the proposal Petey withdrew a distance from the scene for awhile.

Bridie and Aggie went to Lough Derg on pilgrimage.

'I hope they get something out of it,' said the mother.

Lough Derg pilgrimage was no longer a place where sinners went to do penance, but almost entirely made up of three classes of suppliants: First, girls with – as Tarry observed – long noses and flat chests went to pray for husbands; then shopkeepers who had sons and daughters at school and college went to pray that these would pass their examinations; the third class were those who went to pray for health, for themselves or their relatives.

Before going off the mother had asked them to pray for a 'special intention' of hers.

The mother was out at the gate talking to Charlie and when she came in she was agitated. She poked with the pot-stick for her best shoes under the table and brought the polish down from the mantle-board.

'Had a mind to go as far as the town the morrow,' she said in an urgent manner.

'Good God!' said Tarry.

He was too busy at that moment watching the movements of Molly as she crossed the field beyond the meadow to gather the full meaning of his mother's anxiety. Another day dawned.

The mother was dressed for the town. She came out into the street walking with her umbrella and lingered thoughtfully a moment as if she had forgotten something.

Her son was greasing the cart outside the carthouse, dreaming over the fine job he was making of it.

'Don't forget to clean that drink for the cattle in the Low Place,' she said, 'there was a green scum on it that was a total dread the last time I saw it.'

Tarry leaned his chin on the top of the red dashboard and was looking into the body of the cart admiring the new sheeting. That cart was as good as the day it was made four years ago. It wasn't a small cart but it was as handy a cart as ever was made, the sort of cart that you could bring to the town and not be ashamed of. He had the seat-board under the heel at the back so that one of the wheels was off the ground.

He plastered on the black grease with a table knife and then dropping the knife on the ground shot the wheel in on the axle. The sun glanced over the top of the front-board.

'Don't leave that knife there behind you,' said the mother.

'Don't you know very well I won't?' he snapped.

'And you might clean out them hen houses and whitewash the roosts; the roosts need to be whitewashed once a week in the summer. I better be going.'

She went out the gate. 'You might wish me luck,' she said.

'I did wish you luck,' he said, 'but just to satisfy you, "Good morning and good luck".'

'Thank you, and mind yourself till I come back. And keep this gate shut, Tarry, I see that hungry sow of Callan's prowling down there at the turn.'

As she went down the road he could feel the power of her ruthless organizing mind trying to throw a flame over his life.

She couldn't see that apparent indifference and laziness was not laziness but the enchantment of the earth over him, and the wonder of a strange beauty revealed to him.

She only laughed and said he was talking like a 'Presbyterian minister'. 'Lazeness, that's all it is, lazeness, lazeness, lazeness.' That was what she said hundreds of times and he had no answer. She went round the turn and out the main road and watching her from the gate he knew that she was spreading her mind over the fields and the years.

She was going to the town this day to inquire about the sale of the major part of Carlin's farm, seven fields which were not part of the holding of two acres upon which the house stood. For many years this farm had been 'up on the wall', but nobody was anxious to be the first to bid owing to the savage threats of two cousins, Tommy Finnegan, whose land bordered the Carlins', and his brother, Larry, who had once been a famous footballer and as a consequence had the reputation of being a 'good' man – that is good in a drunken brawl.

But something had recently happened to lessen the moral force of these two men who claimed to be relations of the Carlins – Larry had been charged with stealing sleepers.

His sister, Mary, poured thick milk into a pan for the hens to drink.

'These ones had a good dry night last night for the Lough Derg,' she said. 'I wonder would you take them two cans, Tarry,' said Mary, 'and go to the well for water.'

Mary had her face washed and was dressed as if she were going to the village. Tarry took the cans after a while, having as usual 'taken the good out of it' by saying he would not.

He walked slowly, dreaming, along the narrow path that skirted a deep sunken stream on the steep sides of which grew primroses in wildest profusion. At the well he lingered, in the cool shadows where a big blue fly buzzed about.

He filled the cans full flowing, for he always took pride in bringing home all the water the cans could hold.

Returning, thinking of the possibility of his coming into the possession of a new farm of land, he stopped for a moment to let the greed of his mind enjoy the full pleasure of ownership. And his mother might get it for a small sum. He often heard it said that the Land Commission would let a man have a farm by merely paying the arrears of Annuities. Wouldn't it be marvellous if she got it for forty or fifty pounds? It was worth close on three or maybe four hundred. That's what would madden Eusebius and all the other greedy people.

He lowered his eyes from staring at nothing and happening to glance towards a clump of nettles, thistles and pigs' parsley that grew at the bottom of the field behind the house, he thought he saw something white moving there.

He laid down the cans and wandered quietly in that direction.

Holies! He could hardly believe it. His sister, Mary, was sitting in the middle of the clump with the tall slick young fellow with the well-oiled hair that he had sometimes seen at the dance hall and disliked because he was such an expert dancer.

He could tell from the soles of her shoes that it was really his sister. He could not mistake that square patch on the middle of the sole which she had herself put on. He couldn't see the girl's face for he judged from a distance of some twenty yards that she had her face screwed behind the fellow's neck. She was in a twist.

This fellow always did his courting in the middle of the day, which was normal enough as he was unemployed.

He watched for a few moments and returned to his cans to find that the foal had put its hoof through the bottom of one. This disturbed him but not as much as his sister's being in the nettles with a scamp from the town. Tarry began to sing because he felt that his voice would awaken his sister to a consciousness of respectability. Noise and shouting show that everything is open and aboveboard.

The rough and tumble is very moral.

Peeping through the hedge at one point he could now see his sister sitting upright but showing no sign of having been seriously disturbed or awakened to a realization of her position.

He was about to put water in the kettle to make some tea for himself when Mary entered, carrying what she said was a dozen eggs which she found down in the nettles at the bottom of the back field. Tarry, who had an eye of embarrassing keenness for seeing what he ought not see, saw that these alleged eggs looked very like small field stones to him.

'I'll blow that wheel,' said she. She was in the best of humour.

Tarry sat at the table and began to speak in a very sing-song preachy voice about civilization, particularly about ancient Celtic civilization and how it gave honour to women's virtue. He was almost repeating one of Father Daly's sermons, and in much the same manner too. He spoke as if he were addressing a congregation and not an individual. As he preached he felt that weariness which bears down on those who are trying to overtake their own arguments. He knew that he was making a cod of himself, but the force of the emotion carried him along.

'All this foreign dancing and music is poison,' he said. 'It never belonged to this country.'

His sister for answer took a cigarette out of her pocket and lit it with a live coal. 'What the bleddy hell are you trying to say?' said she.

'You know damn well what I mean.'

'Ah, dry up and don't be making a barney balls of yourself. A person would think you were a missioner.'

'And smoking, too,' Tarry growled.

'Amn't I as much entitled to smoke as you? Give us down that tay canister. I'm as well have a bit of gas while I can.'

'You're gone to hell all right,' said Tarry.

The cup of tea softened his anger. 'Supposing Petey saw you, wouldn't that be a fine how-are-you?'

'Do you know what,' said the girl, taking her brother in hand, 'fellas like you that never as much as had their arm round a woman always think that there's nothing in a bit of a court only the one thing. That's all's in your heads.'

'But what about Petey? Are you ever going to marry him?'

'Do I look out of me mind?'

'Ah, but you shouldn't be making a fool of yourself, having the neighbours talking. What need I care?'

'Codology. Are you looking for a fag? I have a couple here. I'll give you one.'

'I tell you I have one of my own somewhere,' said Tarry, searching in the lining of his jacket. 'I know I ought to have one. No, I don't want your fag.' But he had his hand out for the cigarette as he said these last few words, and taking it was thereafter bought over.

As they were finishing their cups of tea they saw Mary Reilly coming down the road on her bicycle.

'Isn't she very nice?' said Tarry to his sister.

'Isn't she only a lump of dung like the rest of us? Go on out and stop her and hear what she has to say. Go on, I say or you'll miss her. Is it her? It is. I thought it might be Eileen Cassidy that's home from England. Make a rush at it the same as if you were taking a dose of salts. Sure she can't take a bite out of you.'

Under the stimulus of his sister's encouragement Tarry wandered towards the gate and went onto the road and looked sharply in the hedge as if he had lost something.

'Hello!' he shouted before his courage failed him.

'Hello!' she answered very sweetly and got off her bicycle.

He could hardly believe it. The girl he had dreamed of was standing beside him and apparently delighted with his company. There was a humming in his ears and he could hardly hear what she was saying. She said that she saw the poem he wrote in the local paper and that it was 'simply wonderful'. Before she had time to say more he had started off on a tour of English literature, as much as he knew of it, from Chaucer to Yeats. Once more he was delivering a fantastic lecture to a girl. She listened in astonishment. He tried to convince himself that he was doing well, that he was making a deep impression, but something else told him that he was talking too much. He could remember that he had run on like this before when trying to impress girls and while it was immediately successful, none of the girls took him seriously afterwards. He wished he could stop and be at ease. To add to his nervousness he knew that his sister was listening in the doorway picking up the makings of a laugh at him. In the end he did manage to stop lecturing and drifted a few yards away from the gate down the road, with the girl wheeling her bicycle beside him.

'You can play the piano,' he said.

'I'm no good at it,' she said.

'Would you ever come down this way some evening till we have a talk?' Afraid that he had been too bold he hurriedly said: 'I was only joking.'

She gave him a glance that nearly made him faint into the ditch. No girl had ever looked at him like that before.

'What about Thursday evening?' she called back when she had gone some distance on her bicycle.

'Oh, not at all,' he said, without meaning anything of the sort.

He was talking to himself in the deepest distress as he returned to the house. 'You didn't say "not at all",' he groaned. He whispered in his most lyrical manner, 'Yes, dear, Thursday evening at eight.'

'Now,' his sister cried in triumph, 'what did I tell you? She's mad for you. Didn't I hear her?'

'Ah, don't bother me, don't bother me, don't bother me,' Tarry cried. 'I never want to hear another word about it.'

Tarry took the shovel and went off to clean the drinking place for the cattle.

'Well?'

'Well?'

Brother and sister spoke as one as soon as the mother arrived.

The woman plopped to a seat by the window and said: 'Mary, will you throw a shovelful of oats to them hens and not have them picking at the window the same as if they never got a bite. I'm not able to give me sowl to God or man with the heat of that day. Tarry, did you see about the cattle?'

'I did. How did you do?'

The mother ignored the question and said: 'From now on you'll have to change your gait of going.' The woman scrutinized her son's face. 'Is that a scratch on the side of your jaw? Lord! but I can't let you out of me sight but you're liable to do yourself harm, break your neck or something. Mary, pull over that kettle and don't wet the tay till I get me breath.'

'But how did you do?' asked the impatient Tarry.

'I'm making you independent of the beggars, Tarry,' said the mother.

'You got it then. How much?'

'How much do you think now?'

'How would I know?'

'Well, make a guess.'

Tarry guessed what he thought was a wild and high guess to please his mother.

'A hundred and twenty.'

'Ah, you're the man that should be sent to buy a thing,' the woman said shaking her head. 'Give me over me handbag from the table. Yes, you're the man that ought to be sent out. Mary, how many eggs did you get the day?'

'Four dozen and two.'

'She found a nest,' said the impulsive Tarry before he had time to think.

'A nest?' said the mother.

'I was thinking of the one she got yesterday,' Tarry explained.

'Have a look at that, you that's the scholar,' the mother said pushing a document in front of her son. 'You may make the tay,' she said to the daughter.

'Two hundred and fifty,' Tarry said amazed. 'Of course it's worth twice that. I only mentioned the hundred and twenty because I thought maybe you got it cheap.'

'Do you know what the place is worth?' the woman said, with her half-shut fist stuck in her jaw. 'Do you know how much the solicitor said he could get for it if the Carlins were out? Hut! man! ... I believe that this Cassidy one is home, Mary. Were you talking to her?'

'No, I wasn't,' snapped Mary.

'She'll get a man this time or lose a fall,' said the mother. 'And for all that she's not a bad girl. Back to England she wouldn't go if she got the chance of a man.'

'She came to the right place,' said Mary, ironically.

'Eusebius offered a hundred,' said the mother. 'That's about all the money they have in spite of the stallion. From now on you'll have to put an inch to your step and quit the curse o' God dreaming.' She was silent a while as she filled her mouth, for the next remark.

Tarry was at first tremendously excited over the purchase, but as his mother spoke and he thought the matter over he began to pity himself. Even with the eleven or twelve acres added to their present farm what would they still be but poor? What chance would he have of marrying a girl like Mary Reilly? The new acquisition only set him up firmly among the small farmers – fixed him forever at the level of the postman and the railway porter. The new farm only drew attention to their real state. A tramp poet would be above him.

'Lord! these shoes had the feet burned off me,' Mrs Flynn said. She had removed her shoes and was walking through the house in her stockinged feet.

' – Not a bad girl at all,' she mused aloud, 'far from it, and I'm sure they'd give her all they have if she got a good take. And mind you, Molly Brady is a good healthy girl that 'id do a bad turn to no man.'

When the daughter was absent the mother turned to her son and said: 'In two or three years it's you that could be the independent man. These ones will be going sooner or later. Whether they get men or not out they'll go at any rate. Let them start an eating house in Shercock or something. And remember, Tarry, it's not of meself I'm thinking. That little place of Brady's would put a real bone in yours – and what's better, would give you another outlet to the big road. If you'd take a fool's advice what you never took instead of the oul' books and the writing you could be richer than the Reillys. Look at Eusebius cutting calves and pigs and every damn thing to make a penny; and Charlie Trainor that 'id lift a ha'penny out of a cow-dung with his teeth. Oh, it's well I know these parties and that's why I'd like you to be independent of the whole rick-ma-tick of them. In troth, you would. Give me over them oul' boots of mine from inunder the table. Troth, you could. Hut, man, I wouldn't be bothered with these ones that you do be talking about – May up here and this Reilly one. Sure that poor girl, everyone belonging to her died of consumption, God protect everyone's rearing. There's seven of as nice a fields up there as there is in the parish. If you give them any kind of minding it's you that could take out the crop. Do you know, now when you have the chance you might do a bit of scouring to that drain and not have us near up to our knees in water in the winter.'

'I'll start the morrow,' said Tarry.

'Lord! but doesn't the years slip by in a hurry,' mused the mother as she stood looking out the open door. 'Lord O,' she sighed, 'it's only this blessed day I was thinking that your father, the Lord have mercy on the whole lot of them, will be dead five years next week. Ah, the Lord may have mercy on them all.' Tarry had slipped upstairs. 'Tarry, where are you?' called his mother. He sat very still, not wishing to annoy his mother, for he knew that she would be annoyed at his going upstairs to what she called 'the curse-o'-God rhyming'. When she left the doorway and went outside somewhere he came down and walked about the street as if he had been outside all the time. He wished he could have been manly and stayed upstairs. This concealment made him unhappy. Later in the evening he climbed Callan's hill and looked across at his new possessions and it looked so small and mean now as his mind considered the epic plains of Louth beyond. And Reilly's big house and huge fields that he could see from here. He was still a beggar. His mood changed again as he came down the hill and he began to think that a man married to Molly could be very comfortable. It would be an easy way.

Wearing boots, without socks, and with his trousers turned up above his knees, capless, and with the old torn shirt open wide at the neck, Tarry was striding through the thistles and rushes of the meadow on his way to clean the drain. The drain was the stream that separated his farm from those of the Bradys and Larry Finnegans In the summer the cress and sorrel spread over the surface of the stream and the roots of flaggers at one point made a floor across it upon which a man could cross without wetting his feet. If the drain were cleaned every summer it would benefit a dozen small farmers all the way towards its source in Miskin.

This was one of the reasons why Tarry felt not perfectly satisfied when he attacked it with shovel and drag. Cleaning the drain was of much more benefit to the Flynns, no doubt, than to anybody else, for it meant that a three-acre meadow would be partly free from flooding in winter. But it *did* do good to others: that corner of Larry Finnegan's where when the drain was choked a horse would be bogged in the middle of summer could nearly be ploughed when the drain was free. But would Larry give a hand? No fear. He might – and it was as much – come and look on at Tarry Flynn up to his knees in the mud and might even pass comments on the fact that Tarry was shovelling all the mud on to his own side.

Larry's main interests looked out on the main road and he had as a result something of contempt for Drumnay and the methods of the natives in that townland. Tarry meant to spend a few bits of days at the drain before the cutting of the hay and the spraying of the potatoes, and here he was on the first days of July making a rush at the work.

The drag was a specially made instrument which had been bought in Shercock by his mother who had a penchant for old iron. He had an improvised knife for cutting the green scraws; it was made from the blade of an old scythe.

He started at the spot near Brady's well which was the worst spot on the drain. He cut the roots of the flaggers in squares and then began to drag them on to his own bank. It was very heavy work, but he loved it. Indeed, dragging the drain was one of his favourite jobs, the job that most softened about his burning thoughts and desires.

The heavy squares of flagger roots yielded very slowly to his strain. They carried a huge backside of oily mud that was sometimes a hundred weight. Bit by bit he dragged it up the bank and as he eventually landed it safely he was filled with deep satisfaction. The pool left behind by these sods was like a clear well. It was in the long run easier to clean the drain where the flaggers were than at other places, for although the roots of the flaggers were hard to cut and had a high hydraulic soakage, once you had them out you had that part of the drain cleaned.

The purchase of the farm meant that none of his sisters would get a fortune. It would take some doing to get the two hundred and fifty, never mind fortune the girls.

He was leaning back on the handle of the drag, slowly sliding a mighty square of dripping roots and mud upwards and upwards. He slipped on his backside and wet the seat of his trousers.

He had to get a new grip of the sod so he stood up for a moment beside the poplar and took a breath.

Man alive, he was getting on gallant.

Molly stood on the height above him and stared through the sunlight at him but he wasn't interested in her.

The wild bees which nested in the swamp on the other side of the drain filled the air with their hum. A couple of crows descended from the parched sky and landed in Tarry's plot of turnips. He walked up the field from the drain and gave a look at his turnips. He was satisfied; no natural crow would be able to pull one of those turnips.

Tarry's face was half covered with mud from wiping the sweat off with wet muddy hands. If Mary Reilly saw him now what would she say? Not that at that moment he'd care, for now he was hot with a profounder passion ... Even all the work he had done in that bit of a morning would tell in the meadow in winter. A powerful job.

He stopped and pulled a small scraw up with his hands like a man rescuing a drowning person by the hair of the head. He clapped the sides of the dreeping bank with his palms and had a mind to set down and take a rest and a smoke. But not yet. He would do to beside the next poplar and then take a good long rest. A clag rested on the back of his hand and was sucking blood before he had time to kill it.

Molly came to the well for water and they had a few quiet words. The girl looked at the work he was doing and thought it a very good job.

She was dressed in her most seductive raggedness – big rent in her flimsy blouse, cotton skirt that clung to her fat thighs emphasizing contours of sluttish appeal – but he was not thinking about her. He had other things on his mind.

'Man, that's a dousing job,' she said.

'If I had time . . .' he said.

'Do you know what it is,' said he looking along the drain, 'if about six inches was taken off the bottom there at the cutting it would lower the bog till you could nearly lough it. The only trouble is you'd get no one to help you, and when you'd do it they'd hardly give you credit for it. Sure, the McArdles object, saying that the drink for their cattle runs dry when the drain is cleaned.'

Tarry continued explaining the state of the drainage in that area and Molly showed that she was capable of appreciating the fine points of the subject.

'That's the kind of people in this country, Tarry.'

'Molly, did you fall in the well?' called Molly's mother.

The woman needn't have been worried about her daughter on this occasion and Tarry derived much pleasure and moral strength in the woman's misjudgement.

'Wonder, yous are not up at the new place, Tarry? Your mother got a good bargain in it.'

'She gave the full value for it if I know anything, Molly. They can all go to hell.'

'Me mother was delighted to give the drop to them smart Cassidys. Eusebius is raging.'

'Molly, Molly, Molly, what are you doing down there?'

'How are you, Missus Brady?' Tarry called back, and his voice was full of the courage of the man whose dealing with anybody's daughter has been aboveboard. The woman hidden behind the shoulder of the hill could not mistake it.

'Little the better of you,' she answered Tarry back, and he imagined that there was a disappointment in her voice.

Molly was gone and he was alone again with the mud, the lovely oily mud, and stones of the drain. He cut the scraws in squares again. He spat into the water. An eel wriggled out of the side of the bank trying to get back and Tarry made several futile attempts to stop its course.

The shirt climbed up his back and his braces slipped. The trousers were half off him.

He cleaned his hands in a tuft of grass and sat down on the headland at the ends of the turnip drills to smoke and read the old torn book that he had begun some days before and which he since carried in the hip pocket of his trousers. He stretched his legs across the headland and with his head on a pillow of growing rushes held the book over his eyes and started to read. The poplars and a blackthorn bush kept the sun from him and he was comfortable except for his feet, for his boots were full of water, and some pebbles, too, had got in. So he pulled off his boots and kicked them across the headland into the turnip drills.

The book, which had the first page torn out, was the best book he had read so far; there was something weird about the story although the book had all the appearances of the usual torn faded cheap novels with which he was acquainted. Madame Bovary was a wonderful character, he said to himself. Yet it wasn't her character but the queer difference that was in the book. Good as the book was, he grew sleepy as he lay there and he cast the book aside in the clump of rushes and from a lying position began to think what a curious strange world were these common fields that he knew so well.

The boortree at the other end of the field seemed to be hundreds of feet high. He stared straight up at the sky without a thought in his head. As he lay there, the pad, pad of soft slow footsteps coming along the headland roused him. It was his mother. She was saying:

'Nothing kills me only these buck nuns that make out they wouldn't look at a man, Tarry. Lord, God of Almighty! If you had to hear the giving out to me I got from that Aggie there now you'd think she was made in a foundry. I hope Lough Derg does them some good. You're making a great job of the drain.'

Tarry, vexed with himself to be caught idle after all his hard work, was on his feet now.

'Take your rest, you needn't mind me,' said the mother. Then: 'Is that a miss I saw up there, Tarry?'

'No, that's the little rock,' said Tarry looking round.

'I thought it was a miss. Were you talking to this slob on the hill? I wouldn't tell much to that one, a real gabby guts ... Them spuds will soon need to be sprayed ... Musha, who's is the big foot in the gutter there?'

'Larry.'

'And did he say anything, the dirty oul' rogue?'

'No, he said nothing.'

A car purred slowly up the Drumnay road going very slowly past Flynn's gate in case there might be chickens there and the mother was watching it with some anxiety until it had gone past. 'Bedad,' said she, 'that young priest is nearly living in Reilly's these days. Nothing for these priests but the rich.'

'They say,' said Tarry, 'that he's going to get Mary into some music school in Dublin. She's a great player of the piano and Father Markey is very interested in music.'

'The best thing for the likes of us to do is to keep away from parties like that, Tarry. Does she ever speak to you?'

'Oh, an odd time.'

'That's a very wide headland, Tarry. Do you know she's not nearly as fine a girl as she was a couple of years ago. I told Aggie to bring you over a sup of tay as soon as the big pot comes off the fire. Aye, too,' she said to herself about nothing.

She turned round and began to walk slowly back, and as she came along Tarry could see that she had some important advice to give him. 'Whatever you do don't go up there for the present. You'd get a false kick or a prod of a graip, and that's what 'id please Eusebius. They'd all love to see a good row now. Big Lip Larry over there is making out to be a friend of theirs; he's not a full fourth cousin. I'm nearly as close meself. And damn them anyway but sure they're no good to the country. The best of a farm if it was minded. In three or four years you wouldn't know that place if you keep your eye on it ... There's Molly coming to the well again. And that's a warm little piece of land too. And this Molly is no fallen goods either. One of these days you ought to take the cart up there and draw down them two nice ash trees that's on the march with Eusebius – or if you don't, he'll claim them, because they're growing more or less on the middle of the ditch.' The woman moved off slowly and sideways as she looked up the drills.

Tarry's sense of progression in the clear air did not last long. Again the Earth tempted him and for no ordinary reason he found himself walking across the drain over the floor of flagger roots. He stood among the yellow-blossomed flaggers that nodded about his shoulders filling his mind with the emotion of green leaves. Then he moved deeper into the mystery and walked through the swamp to the well.

For no ordinary reason he walked across the drain over the floor of flagger roots and stood among the tall green blades that were up to his shoulders. He liked standing there with the yellow blossoms of the flaggers nodding about him.

He stood for a few moments filling himself with a soft emotion in the mystery of green leaves and then decided to explore further the swamp around the well. It was a long, long time since he had been on this side of the drain. He looked into the well and then lay down on his belly and took a drink of the cool water. A frog leaped in right before him and, poised under the water, looked up straight at him as if making a face at him. He was almost too lazy to get on his feet. The heat of the day had blotted out his mind. Here was a bees' nest. It would be a good idea to get the honey. This ought to be a good year for honey.

He sat by the edge of the drain some distance from where the tools were, idly staring across the boggy hollow which was all a-bloom with flowers the names of which – being a country-man – Tarry did not know. He didn't need to know their names unless he wanted to tell somebody who didn't know about them. But it could be said that he 'knew them by eyesight', and was intimately acquainted with these blue fluffy blossoms whose stems were so juicy, and the hard pink-petalled flowers too. He knew the names of the bogbane and water-violet and the marsh-marigolds, but these names meant little to the man who had the reality. And as he sat there the scents of a thousand flowers and the still stronger scents of the clay at the roots of turnips buried him in a fog of enchantment. Only one part of his being was alive on the common earth. The more he was involved in the earth's enchanting mist the more did his imagination wander among the lusts of the flesh. He wondered would Mary Reilly come down on Thursday evening, which was the next evening. With her he felt so good too. He dragged himself out of the fog and stood on the bank trying to shake himself fully conscious.

Molly was coming to the well for more water. It amazed Tarry the amount of water the Bradys used. Now, said he to himself, just because I don't care one way or the other, we'll see what she'll say.

'Are you mad?' she bawled when he made a grab at her. 'Let me go.' She caught his thumb and nearly broke it in two. That convinced him that he had made a mistake. Dirty ragged women can be quite moral. But was Molly moral? He would like to find out. He was sure that when she came to the well again she would ignore him but he was wrong in this. She was more friendly than ever.

Another day came hot and close, and after breakfast he cut a sheaf of fresh hay for the mare which, with her foal, was being kept in a field that was bare enough of grass, because this field was the safest for the foal, with no wire palings in which he could get entangled. He hung the scythe in the hedge at the gate of the hay field as it was an old scythe that could safely be left out. People weren't in the habit of stealing farm tools, though one never knew.

His boots, which he had left outside the door during the night on account of all the mud which was on them and in them, were still nimble with damp when he put them on. Once again he thrust his trousers over his knees and headed for the drain. With his feet in the wet boots, the dry clay and stones under them produced in him the sensation of being naked. He felt like a man in football togs. There was something illogical in the dry clay, so dry and yet his feet slipping inside his boots. When he got to the drain, and water and mud met water and mud, he felt more at home.

On this day his work took him to a part of the drain where shovelling was more necessary than the drag. He had a plank across the drain which he stood on as far as possible, but in general he had to go down into the muddy drain and work with a short grip on his shovel.

In spite of everything, the close heat of the weather and the blood-sucking clags, those days in the drain were some of the happiest days of his life.

> 'As I crossed McArdle's field I wondered
> As I looked down into the drain
> If ever a summer day should find me
> Shovelling up eels again.'

There were scores of eels in this section. Tarry skinned one but found its snaky, slimy body so disgusting that he did not bring it home to put on the pan. He kept the skin, as the skin of an eel was supposed to make a good strap for the wrist and prevent a man getting a cramp in it. He had some difficulty getting all the mud shovelled on to his side for there was a thick hedge on his own side, but he cut holes at intervals of a few yards through which he was able to pitch the mud. The land on the other side was the remains of a cut-away bog which had belonged to different people when the bog was a bog. Who owned the part of the bog at this point would only be discovered in cases of a bitter argument among the neighbours.

Tarry cut the scraws wide here so as to have plenty of mud. The sides of the high bank were held together by the roots of the bushes and there were wasps' nests and rat holes, and there were also violets growing in the moss as high up as if on the side of a mountain, it seemed to Tarry, sunk in the drain. He threw up a round stone and a dead cat, and an old enamel teapot, and dreaming into these finds he was an explorer.

'There's another egg here, will you eat it, Tarry?'

'Sure, two's any god's amount.'

'Devil the damn harm it 'ill do you. Go on and throw it into you, you're working hard.'

'And I only ate the bare one egg that was only like a cock's egg,' said Aggie, from the corner.

'And it's plenty for you,' replied the mother quickly. 'Keep you from going madder for the men.'

'Men, men, men,' sighed Aggie, 'there's nothing in your grey oul' head but the men. You'd nearly take a man yourself.'

'And in troth,' said the mother rather pleased, 'I'd get a man quicker than any of yous – as ould as I am. Aye, would I. Devil a good Lough Derg did you.'

'Oh, look at her now with the claub of laughing on her face,' Aggie said referring to her mother, who had taken a fit of laughing as she picked at a rind of bacon in the doorway.

She threw it to the hens, which made a great helter-skelter in pursuit, and said: 'Three lovely daughters and if the Lord hasn't said it they'll be stuck like a blind to me window all the days of me life. Tarry, there's a two-shilling bit there on the dresser you might want for fags.'

'He stole my one and six that I had hid in the flower-pot,' said Bridie. 'If you hid money in the river that fella 'id find it.'

'Grin away, grin away,' jawed Bridie. 'Trying to make out you're the good boy, trying to look holy when the Reilly one does be about, one that would water on him. Oul' cod!'

'Go lang, you slut, you,' said the mother with effect. 'If he took it atself, who had a better right to take it? Sure it's not yous with your painting and powdering and God-knows-what.'

'But the point is I didn't take it,' said Tarry.

'Oh, no, wouldn't know how.'

'Pass no remarks of her like a good fella,' said the mother. 'I suppose,' said she changing the subject, 'you'll be cutting that piece of hay above the rock in the Low Place tomorrow or the next day. You'd smash a mill there on the stones.'

'I suppose I'd be better get it out of the way before the spraying of the potatoes.'

He was combing his hair at the mirror. First he combed it straight back in the manner of those expert dancers from the slums of Dundalk and other distant towns who were to be seen at the hall every week. Then he changed his mind and his hair style and swept it to the side. He put a dreamy expression in his eyes. Was he good looking or does every man admire his own face? His mother and sisters were never done saying what an 'ugly-looking animal' he was, and he being highly sensitive this criticism weakened his self-confidence.

This was Thursday evening. Would the girl come?

Outside it was threatening rain. He half hoped it would rain and give him an excuse in case he happened to be disappointed.

'Surely you're not going away this evening?' said the mother coming in from the gate, 'and that heifer liable to calve any minute. And them three sheets to galvanize in the street, you should put them where the mare or foal would not be in danger of cutting themselves. And the good shoes on!'

He was tired but it was a pleasant tiredness in the small of his back and in his arms. He went into the cart-house and put on a collar and tie as he did not want to attract too much attention. Bridie was coming through the meadow with the milk as he went out the gate and he hurried in case she might have news that the heifer was near calving time.

He stood on the middle of the main road at the entrance to Drumnay. The only people on the mile of road from the cross-roads on one side to McArdle's gate on the other were three of the Dillon girls, with dozens of men waiting for them. Mother a Protestant, they were reared pagans. The two youngest were among them, but now dishevelled and dissolute. Changed since the time before the Mission, when Tarry had desired them. He wouldn't like to be seen talking to them now and hoped they wouldn't try to be familiar.

Tarry walked slowly towards the old road that had once been a great highway between Dublin and Derry. It branched off the main road about a hundred and fifty yards from the mouth of the Drumnay road, and ran up a sharp hill all dressed in the greenest of grass. Briars shook hands across it, and in the middle were stunted blackthorns that goats had nibbled. Scraps of tin, the signs of a tinkers' encampment, were strewed about the grass. The Dillons did not frequent this paradise of courting couples, but brought their men friends into their house and to the railway slopes.

May Callan who was 'doing a line' with a young fellow from the town appeared on the old road with her boy friend, their heads bobbing among the whins and blackthorns, and then sank out of view. Tarry was not worried about May for he thought her the type who was well able to look after herself. In common with men of all simple communities Tarry sometimes took a violent interest in the moral welfare of the local women – and at one time it was about as much as a strange man's life was worth to be caught speaking to one of the girls of Drumnay. In the next townland of Miskin which was more remote and traditional the order still prevailed, with the result that the natives of that district were crooked and inbred as the blackthorns that the goats had nibbled.

'I'll count a hundred,' said Tarry to himself, 'and by that time Mary will have arrived.' So he counted a hundred. At ninety he slowed down his count and at ninety-nine he held the number in suspense for fully five minutes. Then she appeared on foot.

The conversation opened in the normal way:

'Hello.'

'Hello, Tarry.'

The way she used his Christian name fluttered Tarry's heart to little blown bits like leaves in a wind. Her voice caressed him.

'I wasn't expecting you,' he said.

She just looked at him as she had looked once before, and he was quite helpless. But not completely. Automatically he said in a super-objective manner: 'I was just thinking of going up this old road when you came – '

They walked, threading their way among the bushes and briars and over rabbit burrows and the greasy stumps of long-felled trees.

'Marvellous weather,' said he with all the passion of a lover.

'Terrific,' she said.

'Look at the rabbit,' he said, continuing his love talk. 'Give me your hand and I'll give you a pull over that gripe.'

He pulled on her hand and having landed her over the soaking trench let go of her hand. He felt that it was up to him as an honourable man not to get a set-in in that way. Afterwards he was mad with himself. It would be much harder to make a second attempt.

94

They climbed up the hill and through a narrow gap which looked north over Miskin and away down through the dark valleys of Lisdoonan. Almost below them in the hollow was the Parochial House. Father Daly was walking through the field beside the river carrying a golf club on his shoulder.

'You were often in the Parochial House?' he said. 'I never was.'

He did not wait for a reply to this but hurried on to talk about the crops and more weather lore.

'Aren't them nettles very vicious looking?' she said.

He delivered a short lecture on the various kinds of nettles. The sun slanted low and the song of the blackbird thrilled the evening. To the left of them below they could see Petey Meegan come from behind a hay-stack buttoning his trousers. A moment later he was seen putting the lock on his door and dragging himself over the fence as he went on his way to Flynn's. At the same moment they could hear the voice of Tarry's sister, Mary, whispering to her town lover among the briars below them.

A corncrake screeched in Kerley's hay field. In the distance could be heard the rattle of tin cans being left down on stones outside some door. Some woman's voice came across the valleys: 'Drive them calves to the field, Joe.'

'That's a clouting evening for the spuds,' said Tarry.

'Do you think so, Tarry?' the girl said. 'Sit down here.'

He found himself sitting beside her. But he was ill at ease. One part of his mind told him to run, that to be great he must run away from things like this. He knew it was fear, a deep instinct that he could never hope to hold this girl.

Through the bushes he could see the corner of one of his new fields and the sight shamed him when he compared it with the broad tree-lined fields of Reilly's which spread out in the distance.

'I think your new farm is wonderful,' she said as if knowing his mind. 'Here, sit on the tail of this coat.' She spread her coat on the dewy grass and now he was sitting closer than ever he had sat to a girl before. And it was the girl he had dreamt of. He was terribly unhappy, thinking of an hour ahead when it would all be over. Now he was in the company of one who belonged to the highest society of the parish. What would Eusebius say? He would try to make a jeer of it, for that was the kind of Eusebius.

Mary Reilly was so different from Molly who had twisted his thumb and left him more exhausted after his struggle with her than he would be after a day's mowing with a scythe or a day carrying a knapsack sprayer.

She twisted a briar that hung over his head and wound it round a whin root.

'It's a powerful evening,' said he.

He had his hand on the bank behind her within one inch of her back. He would give a good deal to have the courage to move his hand one inch. Eventually he took his hand away altogether.

'You must come up to our house some evening,' she suggested.

'Oh, God! no,' he cried, the offer being too good to be true. 'Sure Father Markey and everybody does be up there.'

'What harm?'

'Oh, I don't know,' he said petulantly.

'You must make a poem for me some day, Tarry.'

He shook his head from side to side. 'Sure I do only be at that for a cod.'

'My! Father Markey thinks you great.'

Tarry was afraid to hear more on that subject though at the time he did not know the reason.

'Were you never talking to him?' she asked.

'I never was talking to a priest in me life,' he said truthfully.

'He has a brother who writes plays,' said she.

'Holies!'

The girl had shut her eyes softly and was leaning her head towards Tarry. Tarry instead of yielding stiffened himself and she straightened up. 'We'd better be getting back,' she said.

They passed Mary Flynn and her lover in the briars as they came down the hill. The girl went round by the main road on her way home. Tarry, talking to himself, walked home alone.

5

Life was too heavy on her feet in that place to leap dramatically when something apparently exciting happened.

The purchase of the new farm might seem to have given the Flynns a new outlet for their emotions, but the reality kept them sober. The only thing which might be said to give a kick of drama to the event was the fact that by all accounts their new next-door neighbour, Joe Finnegan, was lepping mad at the Flynns' buying of the place over his head. Mrs Callan 'who never brought a good story in her life' informed Mrs Flynn that Joe Finnegan, drunk in the village the previous evening, had been threatening to make it hot for the Flynns.

'The man is mad,' said she to Mrs Flynn.

'And who, musha, did he say all this to?' asked Mrs Flynn.

'It's only what I heard,' drawled the woman.

'Bad luck to him, himself and his five pratie-washers,' said Mrs Flynn. The 'pratie-washers' were the five daughters, Joe having been blessed with no son.

When she told Tarry about it he laughed and said he'd break Joe's neck if he as much as opened his gob.

'That's the very thing you mustn't do,' advised the mother. 'That's what some of these cute customers like Eusebius would like. And the best thing would be not to go up at all the day afraid of the worst. Wait till the morrow, the fair of Shercock, for Joe is likely to be there. You can fence the gaps on the march between us and him when there's no one about. The easy way is the best way.' Tarry put the point of the bill hook on the bar of the gate and commenced filing the edge with great energy. 'A man has to take the bull by the horns sometimes,' he said. 'I'm telling you I will.'

'I don't give a damn,' said Tarry with petulant bravado.

The mother peeped over the wall and looked down the road.

'These ones are worse since Lough Derg,' she remarked. 'And,' added she as she wandered through the street, 'I hope they get men out of it. Wouldn't it be a good thing now that you have the hook sharp to go over to the Low Place and trim them briars that's creeping through the new grass and not have the hands torn of ourselves when we're pulling the hay for the cattle … Ah ha, good morning, Charlie, it's early you're on the go.'

'Good morning, Mary. I was just going up as far as Cassidy's; I hear they have a few stores for sale.'

'You must expect a dear fair the morrow, Charlie?'

'I have to take chance on that, Mary.'

'Hurry over, Tarry, and get that job done and maybe you might go as far as the fair the morrow and see if you could get something. A man always learns in a fair' – she was addressing Charlie now – 'but this man of mine, there's nothing for him when he goes there, only the face stuck in a book. Sure, that's no way, Charlie, for a man that means to have a thing. No fear of you reading a book.'

'Oh, your man is going for the big money.'

'Bunk,' gasped Tarry from the vicinity of the hen-house door. A fellow like Charlie could think of nothing only money.

'Come home early for your dinner,' the mother called as he went down by the meadow gate with the fork and billhook on his shoulder.

The conversation of his mother and Charlie at the gate pursued him as he went through the meadow where the clags and white butterflies were dancing in the sun. Did a man like Charlie ever notice the butterflies? That man was wise in the ways of the world. But wasn't it easy being wise in that small way. The meanest minds became the great ones of the world's wisdom because the really fine minds saw that such success wasn't worth while. Politicians, businessmen and all that breed could be beaten blind at their own game if the good men tried. He was quite sure of that.

This field ran along Brady's on the far side of their house and forming a right-angle to the main portion of Flynn's estate. It was reached by a wooden bridge made of trunks of pine trees and covered over with stones and clay. In this field Tarry was cut off from the activities of Drumnay. He could daydream here without being disturbed. The sounds of the country people came through the blue haze of the air and the green leaves of the hedges sieved, fine.

There was a defect in him which these secluded fields developed: he was not in love with his neighbours; their lives meant little to him, and though off his own bat he was a very fine thinker and observer he had only one pair of eyes and ears and one mind. Had he loved his neighbours he would have the eyes, ears and minds of all these, for love takes possession.

Christ was the sum of the wisdom of all the men for whom He died, which was the race of Man.

He loved the fields and the birds and trees, stones and weeds and through these he could learn a great deal – but hardly enough. He saw the centre as a poet sees, but this introversion was leading to aridity. Men impacted themselves on him almost against his will. If he had been entirely passive he might have become wise. But he screamed hysterically when the lover wanted the beloved to sleep. He tore the emotion horribly.

The mother did not understand this queer kink in him which she felt would lead him to destruction. She would merely shrug her shoulders and say: 'I might as well be talking to the wall.'

Through the thick hedge he could see into Brady's street and when the door was open hear the talk within the house. It was surely fascinating talk for those who had the faith to see it as the expression of the divine gift of life. As it was, Tarry listened bored, his one and only thought being the seduction of the girl. This desire came between him and the romantic vision so that he only heard a confused murmur. Then he pricked his ears.

Mrs Brady came out to feed the hens and she interrupted her 'chuck, chucks' to remark to the daughter, 'I hear the Flynns are after coming from Lough Derg.'

'Aye, they're home.'

'Oul' crooked Petey may come to scratch now,' the woman said with a loud laugh. 'Chuck, chuck. If I was a man I wouldn't marry her if her backside was studded with diamonds. Peter and her is well met, Molly.'

'They are,' drawled Molly.

The mother stooped low and began to wave her head from side to side in Tarry's direction. 'Do you know what, I thought I saw young Flynn over in the hayfield. A terrible listener, that fella.'

The daughter came out and they both stared in his direction. Tarry stood perfectly still behind the thick hedge.

'There's nobody,' said the daughter.

A little later Molly took a big delft jug and went in the direction of the well. Tarry took a notion that he was very thirsty and hurried down along the hedge where he got through a gap into Brady's field.

'Do you know what it is, I'm dead with the drouth,' he cried ever so casually.

'And a pain in your head for the want of a court,' said Molly, adding the rhyme to a well-known local doggerel.

'Give me the lend of the jug, Molly.'

Tarry sat among the tall rushes beside the well and drank. 'God! I'm dead tired,' he said and lay back. 'Sit down here a while.'

He grunted and sighed for weariness, but still the girl showed no signs of being influenced by his hypnotic suggestions.

'Ah, damn its sowl, sit down, Molly.'

'Deed and I won't. There's nothing for you but the swanks.'

'Ah, damn it sowl – '

' – Father, Son and Holy Ghost – '

'There's your mother,' said Molly.

There was no need to tell him. She was coming slowly along the headland of the potatoes on the other side of the stream walking with the long pot-stick. Tarry grabbed the jug and took a long drink of the cold spring water, saying: 'God! I was very dry. I better be getting back,' he said over his shoulder as he made off while his mother and Molly dropped into conversation.

'Will you shout at that fella and tell him to come back,' said the mother to Molly.

'Your mother wants you,' shouted Molly.

'Did someone say something?' said he turning round.

'Have you them briars nearly trimmed?' asked the mother. 'If you have you'd better come home for an early dinner; there's a job I want you to do.'

Tarry trimmed a few long briars here and there to satisfy his conscience and then went home to a dinner of new potatoes and butter.

Coming in from the road gate the mother said: 'Three years ago I said that that man was near the pension age but nothing would do you only that he wasn't passing fifty. And there it's gone now, one of the best jobs in the parish.'

'Who wants to be a postman?' said the fox about the unattainable grapes.

The two girls had arrived home from their pilgrimage and were making up now for the loss of three days' food.

'Sour as a pair of buck weasels,' said the mother.

'All because we haven't the gossip of the world home with us,' pouted Aggie.

'Hurry up with your dinner,' said the mother to the son, 'and fence the gaps between us and Finnegan's so that we can put the cattle on it. Joe, the greedy dog, went and cut a darling ash tree that was growing on our side of the march and if we had the cattle up it would be an excuse to go up every day.'

'Isn't that what I said this morning?' said Tarry.

And so on they talked and argued.

For the second time since the buying of the farm Tarry felt himself elevated by its adventure-possibilities. As he walked up the road he was a hero going forth to conquer. A new world was opening to him. New fields all his own. He would be next thing to being a Louthman, and that's what would make the beggars jealous.

It began to rain. That was a good thing, for Joe Finnegan would be more likely to remain near his house. He hurried up the road past Cassidy's house but as he expected he did not get past unknown to the mother, who stuck her head around the jamb of the hen-house door and measured him up and down.

Possession gives a new beauty to things and Tarry walking through the long grass and weeds of those fields was filled with a satisfaction that was different from the joy he got in gazing over the general landscape. These fields were his. As he strode through the field with the wet weeds lapping about the legs of his trousers up to his knees, a powerful selfishness filled his mind.

He looked at the hedges and calculated the amount of timber on them. He was so pleased too that so many big ash trees had been allowed to remain even when the Carlins must have needed firewood.

The remains of an old dwelling house – relics of the old days when the land was more populated than now – was an added attraction. Before buying this place he would have described that ruin as an eyesore; now he counted the number of loads of good building stones that it contained. He thought of the wonderful job he could make of the yard at home, be able to put a good bottom to it with those stones. A soft peace had descended upon him. The clay, his clay, cooled the desire in his heart.

His thoughts turned to the practical girls he knew and whom he had up to this ignored. He would be happy in that country, happily married with children, and would go to the forge with the horses and converse with the blacksmith, and wander over to the cross-roads of a Sunday afternoon and discuss the football team and politics. He would be among the old men with his hands in his trousers pockets dreaming about the past. Then he would walk slowly home for his tea and the children and wife would be there waiting for him and everything would be as it was in his father's life. How right his mother was! Why should a man seek crucifixion? And that, up to this, was exactly what he had been doing – seeking crucifixion.

Then he raised his eyes to the eastern horizon and he saw the queer light again. But this time he would not be deluded into being one of the Christs whom the world forever seeks.

O clay of life, so cool.

The division between this field and the portion of the farm which ran down the other side of the hill was a clay bank upon which yellow-blossomed whins grew. Flinging his jacket across

102

the fence he walked back a few steps and took a race to the fence to see if he could leap it. His second love had always been athletics and on summer mornings he was usually to be seen running in his stockinged feet round the home farm, over hedges and drains and palings.

He leaped on to the fence among the whins and found himself standing above the world of Drumnay and Miskin and looking far into the east where the dark fields of Cavan fanned out through a gap in the hills into the green fertile plains of Louth.

The rain had stopped and the sun was coming out and the bees and stinging clags were coming alive again.

On the height beyond to the right stood Joe Finnegan's long thatched house. He listened for sounds and his keen ear could recognize from footsteps in Finnegan's street and from the heightened talk that some stranger was there. Like Eusebius. He walked along the march fence between himself and Finnegan's potato field, to see how many trees and bushes had been cut. There was a lovely ash cut down and the fresh stump covered with mud and weeds. That showed that whoever cut it knew its ownership was doubtful. Greedy devils. In fencing the many gaps Tarry was going to make sure that he would cut only those bushes which grew more on Finnegan's side than on his. He'd get what was doubtful first, the law would give him what really belonged to him.

In ordinary circumstances a terrible lethargy descended upon Tarry when starting a job like this. Now the energy of a man who was grabbing something that didn't belong to him urged him on, made him strong, decisive. He kept his eye on the laurels behind Finnegan's house and once thought he had seen one of Finnegan's five young daughters moving between the laurels and the back of the house. There was a lane at the back of the house, the lane which served this part of Carlin's farm and Paddy McArdle's bog field farther up. How glad Tarry was that he didn't have to use that lane.

A few moments after the young girl had disappeared Tarry

heard a wild commotion in Finnegan's street and the violent rattle of buckets being flung down. He also heard the soft retreating footsteps of Eusebius going off by the front of the house. Then the ferocious voice of Joe:

'Bleddy pack of foreigners, bleddy pack of foreigners. I'll break his bleddy neck.'

'Joe, Joe,' his wife appealed, 'be careful, for you know as well as bread that that man isn't like another. If that man was to drive the fork in you there wouldn't be a thing done to him. Look out for yourself for he's not square.'

'I'll make him square, Maggy,' roared Joe. 'Give me that graip, give me that graip. I'll drive it to the handle in him.'

He was wrestling with his wife for possession of the graip.

'The graip 'ill only give him the chance to let your guts out, Joe.'

'By the sweet and living God he's not going to cut my bushes, Maggie. By the living God I'll . . .'

'Joe – '

The wild man appeared at the top of the potato field in his shirt and trousers and clutching his cap in his hand. He raced diagonally down and across the potato drills stumbling among the stalks in the hollow and bawling 'bleddy foreigners' as he ran. He slowed down as he came along the level ground and stopped shouting, but now his face was fierce with a helpless hate. Tarry was afraid.

Joe walked along the hedge, panting, trying to swallow some of the hate that was choking his words. In the end he said in a low poisonous whisper: 'Flynn, I'll get you, I'll get you.'

These words were ordinary enough but they carried a heavy load of danger. Tarry trimmed away at weeds and briars as quietly as he could to keep the continuity of his legality.

The man on the other side of the hedge came up from the depths of his silent fury:

'What the hell do you mane, Flynn?'

Tarry did not reply.

Joe walked a short distance away and examined a bush which Tarry had cut. 'Oh, you hure you, you hure, you, Flynn, and that's what every one belonging to you were. The good big bush!'

Now the man was shouting at the top of his voice. He pranced on the headland and made a dash as if to jump through the hedge, but fell back nursing his skin where it had been scratched.

'If you come out here,' said Tarry softly, 'I may as well tell you, Finnegan, that I'll cut the head off you. Do you hear that?'

Immediately the man had rushed through a gap and went for Tarry. As he rushed at him Tarry, who had studied a book on boxing, dropped the bill-hook and rammed out his left arm in Joe's general direction, half hoping that it would miss him, for he would give a good deal to be able to avoid a fight.

To Tarry's surprise the punch connected with the man's right eyebrow, cutting it right open. The blood streamed down Joe's face. To avoid further fighting Tarry tried to grapple with his opponent and when he did so he was surprised to find that this man who had such a reputation as a filler of dung and a carrier of thirty-stone sacks of wheat, was as weak as a cat.

Joe tried to scratch Tarry's face and what was worse than all he tried to give him the boot in the belly. To lift the boot to an opponent was considered the meanest of all, and any man who did so in a public squabble would be set upon by the rest of the crowd. Next he tried to pick a large stone off the ground but Tarry shoved him away.

Tarry knew now that he could easily beat Joe, but his faith in physical force was weakening and he wished he could scrape out of the argument in some easy way. In fact, although he was winning, he had a strong inclination to run. The blood on the man's face was now running down his shirt front, frightening him more than it did Joe.

Joe looked like a man who was refusing to believe that he, a man who had played football for the parish team and who had the reputation of being the toughest man in the team, could be bested by this – nobody of a Flynn. He fell to the ground but struggled to his feet quickly. He was surviving by the memory of his greatness. With victory so easily won Tarry's fear of the talk that would be about the fight among the neighbours, as well as

105

of the chance it would give people to draw attention to a land dispute that was going on over the farm, produced in him again the desire to run.

He did run right to the end of the field where the old ruins were and expected Joe to follow. But Joe did not follow. Tarry laid the tools across his knees as he sat down on a mossy boulder in the middle of what had once been the kitchen of a cabin and watched Joe in the hollow rubbing with the lining of his cap the blood away.

During this period the wife appeared on the scene coming in a state of terror across the potato drills.

'Joe, what happened to you?'

Joe was now rubbing the back of his head. Would it be possible that the man got injured when he fell? Tarry tried to daydream that the row had never taken place. He tried to place himself back in the past and then forward in the future when there would be no more about the whole business. He was nervous. He wondered what he would say to his mother. He also knew that the unreason of the Finnegans would not let the matter drop; from now on his life would be in danger wherever he went – in pub or fair or at the cross-roads. The Finnegans were like wild animals. If Tarry had only one first cousin atself, he thought, he would be safe enough; but he had not a single relation to back him up.

Oh, as sure as his name was Tarry Flynn a week would not pass before he had heard more about this fight.

Maggy Finnegan led her husband away round the headland, for it seemed that he was too weak to walk through the potatoes.

From the legal point of view Tarry felt that he was safe enough. After all the man had no business coming on to his side of the hedge. And there was blood on the stones to prove it.

'The hard man, the hard man.'

Tarry shifted round on the stone and was face to face with Eusebius who had a spade on his shoulder. 'I'm just going to put in a lock of cabbage where the turnips missed,' he explained, 'and I thought I saw you down here. You're fencing?'

'Sticking a few bushes in gaps, Eusebius.'

'A good bleddy idea.' Eusebius looked in the direction of the battle scene. 'A lot of gaps in that hedge all right – but as the fella said, you have plenty of good strong bushes to do the job. See any women lately?'

Tarry, glad of the chance to keep the subject away from his nerves, entered into the spirit of the sentimental lead, but his enthusiasm was very forced.

'I was talking to May Callan last night.'

'I see,' said Eusebius as if he had heard something very special. 'Had she any stir?'

'If you knew but all!' said Tarry, making mystery.

'Jabus.'

'Charlie followed her from the cross the other evening when she was coming home and tried his best to get her to come out to Kerley's hayfield with him. What do you think of that?'

'Aw, you're a liar?'

Tarry could not fail to observe that Eusebius' attention was not all on the conversation; it was only an excuse to hear all about the row. But Tarry would tell him nothing.

'Begod, Charlie's a quare hawk,' he said without interest, for he was then staring analytically in the direction of Finnegan's house.

'I'd say he was a bad egg,' Tarry offered.

'Oh, the worst – '

'What are you watching, Eusebius?'

'There's a few gaps down there you'd need to stick bushes in, Tarry. If your cattle broke into the spuds after they're sprayed it wouldn't do them any good. Right pack of savages, them Finnegans, aren't they?'

'They're as good as anybody else, Eusebius, if I know anything. Do you ever be up there at all, Eusebius?'

'Do you know, Tarry, I was up with them this morning,' said Eusebius as if admitting something awful. 'Joe borrowed me rope-twister last year and it was as much as he'd give it back when I went for it. That Joe hates me, hates the ground I walk on. There's the oul' one now coming along the lane. Must be going somewhere. She's dressed.'

'God knows where she's going,' said Tarry with great indifference in a tone of deep weariness.

'She has her hat on,' remarked Eusebius.

Tarry was worried. Had he injured Joe seriously? The wife was either going for the police or the doctor or both, he feared, but he did not let Eusebius see his mind. It would be best now for him to leave the fence as it was, in case the police might be coming. So he didn't return to the hedge.

They saw Mrs Finnegan go towards the village by way of the Mass path across the hills. Eusebius took a sudden notion to go back home for something he forgot. Tarry guessed that he was in a hurry home to tell his mother the good news that there had been a terrific row between Tarry Flynn and Joe Finnegan. It was plain to Tarry now that Eusebius had heard and maybe seen the row from beginning to end. He left Finnegan's, Tarry remembered, by the front way and had come around by the front of Carlin's and then appeared on the scene as if by accident.

Tarry stood in the ruins for a few minutes, walking through the nettles and docks and picking at the old mortar near the chimney – in the hope that there might be a secret hoard left there by long-dead misers. Of course he knew that such a hoard was most unlikely, but the idea fed his day-dream of getting very rich. If he could suddenly get rich all his troubles would be solved.

The thought that he had a sack of oats hidden in the old hay in the open shed in the haggard began to get on his conscience. He had been looking forward to selling that sack and having a roughness of money to spend but now such double-dealing seemed unfair to his mother in the battle which she was putting up against the world of Drumnay.

As soon as he went home he promised himself that he'd leave that sack of oats back on the loft.

He put the fork and bill-hook on his shoulder and made for home by the back of Callan's hills where they ran down to the bottom of Petey Meegan's garden where the flax-pit separated Drumnay from Miskin. He needed some moral support and even though Petey was a poor sort of man to have as support, the fact that he had had – and probably still had – a notion of Tarry's sister brought him closer to him than a complete stranger.

The padlock and chain which secured the door of Petey's dwelling were lying on the window-sill, but Petey was out. Tarry was surprised that the careful and suspicious old bachelor who had reached that particular stage of bachelor queerness that he thought everyone was trying to steal from him should have gone off without locking the door. He was probably not far away, possibly in the field. He looked in the window at the kitchen. A pair of yellow boots hung by their laces on the far wall; a rake stood against the dresser, but for all that Petey's kitchen was in comparatively good order. Tarry noted that it had a good concrete floor and that there was an excellent clock on the mantle-board. He wouldn't be the worst take for a girl, and he would be a useful man to have as a relation, so near at hand if a cow was stuck in a bog hole or anything like that. He whistled to announce his presence, and he was gone off and across the drain and was making up the hill towards the top of the green road when he heard Petey's short cough at the door of his house. So he returned to get some consolation and advice.

Petey wasn't too pleased when he heard the story. Joe was his third cousin.

'He's a very thick man,' said Tarry.

'He's a hasty man,' said Petey, 'but I wouldn't say he's a thick man.'

'I didn't hurt him very badly anyway. Are you coming over this evening, Petey?'

It seemed that Petey had changed his mind. 'I might and I mightn't,' said he.

'Well, you'll be welcome, Petey.'

'Indeed, I know that,' he said as if he thought himself the most eligible bachelor in the country.

Tarry left him feeling small enough. As he went up the rushy hill he turned east and could see someone walking about the spot where the row had taken place. It was Joe.

Did he leave something behind him when he fell? Tarry

watched and saw the man go backwards and forwards through the gap. He had a mind to sneak back to see what the man was doing, but he had other things on his mind.

Smoke was rising from Carlin's house; they were getting up. One way of saving a meal.

Tarry gave a last glance towards the place of the battle and there was Joe Finnegan still mooching around like a man who had lost a shilling in the grass. It could be that he was trying to destroy the evidence but if he were he would only make the real truth more obvious. Tarry walked down the hill to his home partly satisfied that he had done his best.

'What in the Name of God way did you come home?' cried his mother who was spreading shirts on the line in the front garden. 'I sent Aggie up to see how you were getting on and she came back to tell me that hilt or hair of you wasn't to be seen, and that the devil the damn the fence you did.' She was disappointed and disgusted with her son.

'But wait till you hear,' he appealed.

'Sure, God and His Blessed Mother knows that I'm waiting and I'm waiting and you're the same as ever you were. No care about anything only the curse-o'-God books.'

'I suppose she didn't tell you that I was attacked by Joe Finnegan and very nearly killed. She didn't tell you that, but she could tell you that I didn't bush the gaps.'

'Arra, what?'

He left the tools against the wall of the cart-house with an air of self-pitying pleasure. 'Only the way I took him it might be a different story,' he said, looking for sympathy.

'The Lord look down on us anyway. And may the devil thrapple that big-mouthed Joe that – that it's no wonder he hasn't a man child about his place. Could he have better luck with his five pratie-washers? And the devil a son ever he'll have. What did he say?'

'It's not what he said, it's what he did or tried to do. Came down rushing at me like a mad bull with the graip in his hand – '

'Lord bless us, the graip. Bad luck to him. And – '

'He came through the hedge and made at me. I had to hit him.

I hit him the smallest little tip you ever saw and he fell. And that's all.'

Mrs Flynn rubbed her marriage ring as if looking for inspiration in it. 'I hope you're telling me the story right,' she said, 'for that man would swear a hole through a ten-gallon pot. If I had me way I'd have sent Aggie up with you and then you'd have a witness, but no – you wouldn't let her go with you, you were too much the big fella. That's the kind of you. And sure, Lord God! what other man but yourself would try to steal the little grain of oats that I was keeping for the hens in the hungry summer. To think that . . .'

Tarry ran away towards the haggard and his mother's words followed him: 'Oh, that's you all over. You don't want to hear the truth.'

She followed him and found him wrestling with the sack of oats. 'Is it trying to rupture yourself you are?' she said. 'Can't you leave it there till we empty a wee lock out of it with a bucket. Lord God! to think of a man trying to leave the hens without a bit to eat in the red raw summer.'

'Will you give us a breeze?' Tarry screeched.

But the mother was relentless: 'And the book in the pocket! Couldn't go up as far as Carlin's to put a few bushes in gaps without the book.'

'I tell you I had no book. I had no book. Do you hear that?'

'There's no use in talking to you, Tarry. You're your uncle all over that the whole parish wouldn't be able to keep in drink and squandering. Just like you he had nothing big about him but the talk. Did Maggy come out?'

'No, she didn't, she didn't, she didn't,' cried the exasperated Tarry.

When he told her how Petey had taken the news she was still more annoyed. The wireless could not have spread the news more rapidly than the gossipers of the place. It was something to keep boredom away. Tarry could not see the funny side of it at all. Some people said it was because he did not care for anyone but himself, and his own self-critic told him that this was the reason.

It is easy to see the beauty and humour of life when one is detached.

Returning from the field where he had been filling spraying barrels with water he found his mother talking to Charlie at the gate. She had just bought two nine-months-old calves from the man and as usual asked her son how much he thought she had given for them. He, as usual, did his best to flatter the animals and his mother's bargaining powers by putting a high value, as he imagined, on the calves. He thought she had given about eight pounds each, so he said nine.

'They may let you out, Flynn,' said Charlie.

'Exactly,' said the mother. 'I often wonder, Charlie, that some people's not millionaires, they're such wonderful people for getting things for half nothing. Change them wet trousers and give us a hand to drive them up to Carlin's. I have a nicely patched pair of trousers on the crook beside the fire.'

'Like deal boards with patches,' complained Tarry when he had put the trousers on.

'They'll do a turn as Micky Grant said about the wife,' said the mother.

As they were getting ready to drive the calves up to the farm a car appeared at the mouth of the road, and as it purred slowly between the poplars they all knew that it was either a doctor or a veterinary surgeon or someone with bad news. It was Doctor McCabe, a young medical man from the town. Charlie raised his hat.

The mother looked at her son disgusted with his manners. 'No fear of you being like another and rising your cap to the doctor. Oh, you were too grand!'

Charlie hadn't heard of the dispute with Joe Finnegan and Tarry didn't want to tell him, knowing that he would find out soon enough.

Passing Cassidy's house they ran into Maggy Finnegan who was carrying a commode which she had just borrowed from Mrs Cassidy; it was an article of furniture which circulated from one sick bedroom to the other in the district.

'Who the hell can be sick?' said Charlie.

'God only knows,' sighed Tarry.

The doctor's car was pulled into the grass field alongside the lane leading to Carlin's and Finnegan's. Driving the calves past the car they saw the woman rushing ahead of them with the commode under her arm. Jemmy Carlin was standing outside his front door craning his neck in the direction of Finnegan's.

'Must be one of the Finnegans,' remarked Charlie.

When they came to the spot where the row had taken place all the signs of the row, blood and stones and torn clothes on the briars, were on Finnegan's side of the gap. Charlie noticed it. 'Must have been murder committed there,' said he.

Tarry would not tell Charlie the facts because he could not trust the calf-dealer and he was still hoping that the whole thing would blow over.

In a short time they had the gaps all fenced and were contentedly walking away when they saw two well-dressed men coming down the potato field towards the hedge.

'What the hell must be the matter?' said Charlie. 'There's a lot of activity going on around here ... You have two good fields, Flynn.'

'Oh, yes,' Tarry said awakening from his tragic reverie.

When they were starting up the van they sighted Larry Finnegan coming along the lane in the direction of his brother's at a gasping trot.

Charlie tried to stop him: 'What's wrong, Larry?'

'Bad news, bad news,' he said in a pant without stopping. 'The brother's dying.'

'That's a terror,' said Charlie.

Next, Mrs Cassidy appeared carrying a white quilt and a blessed candle.

'Isn't it terrible about poor Joe?' she said.

'What happened him?' asked Charlie.

'Oh the less said about it the better; he was hurt this morning and he's very bad. The priest was sent for.'

'Was it a kick from a horse or what?'

'I don't know till I go over,' she said and hurried on, delighted to be in touch with bad news.

That it was nothing but a fake injury Tarry was certain. They wanted to cause trouble and they were succeeding. He had only given the man the slightest little punch and it couldn't be the fall. No, the whole thing was a fake. The Finnegans like most of the poor people of that district were never ashamed to make a show of themselves. They revelled in a dramatic scene. That was the sort of thing that Tarry always wanted to avoid and which by trying to avoid he now ran into with a vengeance.

The news of Joe Finnegan's dying condition was the talk of Drumnay, Miskin and the whole parish of Dargan that evening. Some people said that he had fracture of the skull and that a specialist had been sent for. The report that Tarry Flynn had been arrested was also widespread.

Mrs Flynn was in a terrible state as she paced over and back her kitchen floor, crying and beating her thighs and cursing her son. She cried and clapped her hands and broke into the middle of sentences: 'that me heart's broke, night, noon and morning with a man that's always making little of the priests, won't go to confession or a curse-o'-God thing.'

The three daughters were trying to pacify her by making themselves very busy – attending to the pots, coming in and going out in a hurry, shutting in the hens, sweeping the floor, washing the vessels.

'Everything 'ill be all right, mother, wait till you see.'

'With the oul' book in his pocket and the fag in the mouth and then to think of him taking the bag of oats. Oh, I wish and I more than wish that I had let him go to hell out of here when he wanted to go ... that me heart is as black as your boot with him, the blackguard.'

'Come on in outa that with you,' said Aggie to her brother, who during the outburst sat on the shaft of the cart in the carthouse glancing idly through the pages of the Sunlight Almanac.

'Leave me alone,' he said.

The dog came in and sat at his feet. The dog was the only animal with Christian feelings in that area. He patted the dog and stretched its ears and as he did he forgot the torture that was ripping up his soul and for one moment looking through the

114

half-open door saw the Evening Star over Jenny Toole's and he knew – This worry would pass. The grass would reflect the sun tomorrow and the wings of crows would be shadows upon it.

The blackbird began to sing in the bushes behind the shed. His mother's whine had ceased. Bridie had gone to milk the cows. Tarry lit a cigarette.

Tarry sat by the window sipping his tea without saying a word lest he should start his mother off again. She was leaning over the table at the back window with her rosary beads in her fingers.

Every time footsteps sounded on the road outside Tarry jumped, thinking it might be the police. The police were certain to come if not this evening in the morning. The mother left her place by the back window and went to the parlour where Tarry heard her opening the money box. Shortly afterwards she came up with a ten shilling note which she put in an envelope and said: 'I'm sending that ten shilling note to the Redemptrists the morrow morning if the Lord spares me. And if this blows over you'll have to go to your confession to them.'

Tarry growled but did in his own defeated heart promise to confess his sins and to pray as he never prayed before if he got out of this scrape.

What he was trying to make out now was what he had often tried to make out before – and that was how the most innocent action by him always seemed to have in it the seeds of misfortune. How many times had Charlie Trainor been in rows, had beaten up men in pubs. And Eusebius too, he could get away with anything. Tarry remembered how when they were small boys himself and Eusebius were throwing stones idly at a bottle on a wall and as he flung a stone a cow of Callan's put her head over the wall and got her eye knocked out.

They had been waiting to hear the doctor's car coming back, but at nine o'clock there was still no sign, so they came to the conclusion that he went out by the upper end of Drumnay.

'And now in the Name of God,' said the mother, 'let us all kneel down and say the Rosary – for my special intention.'

The mother had Tarry on the run. He knelt down like a child

115

and answered out loudly and never dozed off at all during the prayers.

'Name of Father, Son and Holy Ghost.' The mother made the Sign of the Cross with the Crucifix of her Rosary and straightened her back away from the low stool at which she knelt. Bridie was already going up the stairs to bed. 'Take that vessel up with you,' said the mother. 'Father, Son and Holy Ghost ... Well, now you be to hurt the man somehow, and you didn't tell me. He'll swear you hit him with the slashing-hook.'

'He must have hurt himself when he fell on the stones; but he couldn't be too bad for I'm sure as sure that I saw him after clearing away the evidence when I left. There wasn't a track anywhere on my side when we were up there this evening.'

'And why the devil's father didn't you tell me that? Oh, Lord God!'

'I'm sure there's damn all wrong with him, mother.'

'Don't I know only too damn well that it's making out he is, but the making out is as bad as anything. He'd like to put us out on the door. I was talking to Molly there and she was telling me that Mrs Cassidy was telling her that there isn't a whit the matter with him. But what good is that to us?'

'The doctor ought to know.'

'The doctor can't tell everything.'

It was morning, and as he walked through the cabbages in the garden while waiting for Bridie to bring home the milk for the breakfast he could not help feeling the gentle cool caress of the cabbage leaves and the dew-wet honeysuckle in the hedge cheering for the lovelier truth that fluttered wings above the mean days.

Considering himself, he found that he had not been seriously hurt in spirit over the trouble with Finnegan, and today he was better prepared to meet whatever challenge came. The snails climbing up the stones of the fence and the rushes and thistles in the meadow beyond seemed to be putting a quilt of peace around his heart.

He went to the village after breakfast to buy the spraying stuff and found the clerks in Magan's were surprised at his being out of jail. The village blacksmith in for a 'cure' came up from the public house end of the shop and told Tarry that if he wanted a witness to stand for him he wouldn't hesitate.

'Only pretending to be hurted, that's all,' said the blacksmith. 'You don't worry, sham-shiting behind the hedge he is.'

'Are you sure of that, Tom?'

'Positive, positive.'

Tarry had gumption enough to remember to stand the blacksmith a drink.

He learned in the village that Mrs Finnegan had been to the police but that they had advised her to prosecute; it wasn't a case for the police.

Cycling home with nearly a hundredweight of sulphate of copper and washing soda on his back he felt less burdened than if he had no load. His mother was pleased when he told her what he had heard and particularly proud of her son having had the sense to stand the blacksmith the drink. 'That's why I like you to have money in your pocket,' she said, 'not to be smoking it and wasting it on oul' books.'

6

Petey called to Flynn's one evening again but he was plainly drifting, or sidling, out of the marriage notion. He was displeased over the beating his cousin Joe had received.

'He's a gelding,' said Mrs Flynn, 'they're all very thick with their relations.'

The neighbourly dislike of the Finnegans for the Flynns had now warmed into vicious hatred. Tarry was not behindhand in his fury: he was continuously either day-dreaming or planning the destruction of Joe and his family. He put himself off to sleep every night for a fortnight on the day-dream that Joe had fallen on the blade of a scythe and severed part of his genital organs.

Then one morning Eusebius brought him word that the Finnegans were rehearsing a court scene in which he (Tarry) was figuring as defendant.

Tarry had often heard it said that all the branches of the Finnegan tribe had always rehearsed court cases in which they were interested in advance, but he accepted the story as a good story, no more. He was too vexed and hated too much now to see any humour in the thing. But one evening as they were coming from the village nothing would do Eusebius only that they should sneak over by Finnegan's house till they'd see.

It was a fine summer's evening and the night air was scented most enchantingly, but so depressed with anger and hate was Tarry that he had no time for either the beautiful night or the enchanting scents. Neither did he observe anything in the vicinity of the house. Eventually they got to the back window and could see in.

The scene going on was like a play. As he remembered the scene later when he was less angry it appeared thus:

Characters:

Mrs Maggy Finnegan . . . . A Judge
Joe Finnegan . . . . A Plaintiff
Petey Meegan . . . . As Tarry Flynn the defendant
Larry Finnegan . . . . Solicitor for the plaintiff
Johnie McArdle . . . . Solicitor for the defendant

(Plaintiff is giving evidence.)

I was coming quietly down me drills of potatoes to see if they were blighted when I saw the defendant on my side of the hedge in a fighting attitude. He had a slashing-hook in his hand.

Solicitor for Plaintiff: You were afraid of the defendant, no doubt?

Plaintiff: I was terrified of him; he is a very peculiar class of a man.

Solicitor: You thought he was about to attack you?

Plaintiff: I was.

Solicitor: You said nothing to anger him?

Plaintiff: I never opened me mouth.

Solicitor: He then attacked you and you tried to defend yourself?

Plaintiff: I did the best I could.

Solicitor: Flynn is a much bigger man than you?

Plaintiff: He's a big bad man; I'd bate the breed of him in any kind of a fair fight.

At this point the court adjourned in some consternation and a general confab took place.

'If you say a thing like that you're bet before you begin,' said one.

'We're better try Flynn in the box before we chuck it,' said another.

Eusebius giggled quietly but Tarry saw nothing funny in the affair.

The wife, who was playing the judge, was now finishing the porridge in the tin porringer which she had on the table beside her.

'Petey, get into the box.'

'I'm ready,' said Petey, without moving from his seat.

The Solicitor for the Plaintiff goes at once into the attack without allowing the Defendant's own lawyer to examine his client directly.

Solicitor: You're a bit of a poet, Flynn, I believe? (laughter).

Petey (attempting to mimic Tarry): There's a great beauty in stone and weeds (more laughter).

Solicitor: Your mother bought a farm for you to keep you from the lunatic asylum, is that the case?

Petey: I admit she bought a farm.

Solicitor: What's known as grabbing a farm, isn't that so?

Petey scratches his head in imitation of Tarry.

'Isn't he the lousy bastard?' commented the real Tarry.

'Howl on,' said Eusebius.

Petey: She gave full value for it, if I know anything.

Solicitor: Would it be any harm to ask you where she got the money to pay for it? (Petey does not reply.)

There was here a second private confab as to the method of attack on the defendant and his family. The judge got up and disappeared for a time.

'Do you mane business at all, Joe?' asked his brother.

'I bleddy well do mane business.'

'Doesn't look like it to me.'

'I have to go out to loose a button,' said Joe.

'Come on,' said Tarry.

'Howl your horses,' said Eusebius.

Tarry wasn't risking being caught and he was already on his way through the dry dust of a dunghill and over the remains of a pit of mangolds.

His mother was gone to bed when he arrived home. She called down: 'Where were you?'

As he heated milk for himself he told her what he had seen.

'And Petey was there?' cried the mother. 'Lord, O Lord! it's no wonder I do be telling you to mind your things with the class of people that's on the go in this country.'

In one way the mother was pleased by this burlesque development; if the Finnegans really meant business, if they really were in a state of blind anger and hate they would be unable to make a play of the theme.

'Petey will hardly ever come back for Mary,' said Tarry.

'No loss,' said the mother. 'Aggie was telling one of the priests on Lough Derg about it and he said she'd be mad to have anything to do with him. He said that it would be a sin for a young girl to marry the man. And do you know, I kind of think he's right. They're thinking of starting an eating-house in the town. Have a better chance of getting a man that way. Since she went to the factory May up the road has scores of young fellas after her. And even if they *are* barefooted gassans at least they're young hardy chaps . . . Drink your drink, sugsie.' She was giving a drink to the calf out of a bucket. 'Take this bucket and bring the calf to the meadow, he'll follow you,' she said.

'Terrible the changes that's taking place, Tarry,' she rambled along musingly.

'Greedy pack. You'll have to keep an eye on them trees or they'll not leave you one to make a swing-tree.'

He took the knapsack sprayer out of the dairy, put it on his back and was going off to finish the spraying of the potatoes when his mother called after him with a small can of milk in her hand. 'I don't want you to be stooping down to drink out of that well; I do be afraid you'll fall in one fine day.'

'Aw, you're . . .' He checked himself, for once not wanting to tear through his mother's affection for him.

Up and down the drills he went. As well as being his day's work this was also an exercise of the will, the will to live and have faith, the faith of a flower or of the sun that rises every morning.

The spray blew like a fine mist through the leaves of the potatoes. Half way up a drill the nozzles choked and he had to blow into them with his mouth. The taste of the copper mixture was in his mouth and his lips were blue. The narrow bottoms of the drills made his feet turn sideways so that he was walking on the edges of his soles.

He had faith in the day and faith in his work. That was enough. Without ambition, without desire, the beauty of the world poured in through his unresisting mind. He backed into the side of the barrel on the headland and let the sprayer rest on the seat-board of the cart which lay across the top. He lit a cigarette but found that the taste of spraying stuff did not agree with nicotine and he had to throw the cigarette away.

All day he sprayed the potatoes, and nothing was happening except his being. Being was enough, it was the worship of God.

When he went home that evening his mother had a pair of dry trousers ready for him to put on. She was a terrible woman for keeping old trousers going. How could a man think of himself as being in love with a beautiful girl when wearing such rags? He had intended putting on his good trousers but he knew that if he mentioned doing so or made the slightest complaint about the raggedness of the other ones his mother would call him everything but a decent fellow. She would probably go into a fit of the tantrums. But the memory of the potatoes was in his mind and the imagination of the clay and weeds and into that picture any pair of trousers would fit him. He was a part of the ragged little fields.

'I just sent Mary up to see about them cattle in Carlin's,' she said as he put on the trousers in the dairy. 'If you didn't keep an eye on your things you wouldn't have them. I don't know what's keeping her. Yes, it pays to keep an eye on your little stuff.'

He had a mind to go over to the cross-roads; it was the only place a man could go in the old trousers he had on – but he changed his mind and went upstairs to his room where he brought out the old American book on phrenology and began to look through the pictures.

Eliza Cook: Poet. 'Mental Temperament, Large.'

Tarry rubbed his fingers round his head, feeling for the bumps of poetry. According to the book the most poetic head was that belonging to an American poet called Clark, of whose works Tarry had never heard. But the people who made the book seemed to think that on the shape of his skull alone he was entitled to be called a great poet – and Tarry was inclined to agree. This poet was ugly enough. The top of his head across the brow was very wide and his chin was very thin. The eyes were large and bulging and it was hard to say whether it was a man or a woman.

But Tarry would have liked to have such a poetic-shaped head. If he had an extra half inch on each side of his temples he would be a great poet too. He got a comb and combed back the hair from his brows. He narrowed his mouth and chin and considering his appearance in the mirror adjudged himself nearly as great a poet as Clark.

He was going through the book examining other mighty heads when he heard his mother's voice at the gate in conversation with Mary Reilly. He put his head out the window where he could see without being seen and there was the girl standing beside her bicycle, dressed in a summery dress which revealed all the contours of her limpid body.

How ashamed of his mother Tarry was! She was making no attempt to be polite. On the contrary she was being worse than usual. O my God! he gasped to himself when his mother ostentatiously blew her nose with her fingers. How could he raise himself in the girl's eyes after she had seen the kind of his mother?

'Is your bike flat?' she asked the girl.

The girl said it was, and then the woman shouted: 'Come out, Tarry, and pump the dacent girl's bicycle.'

He was in a swether whether or not he should wait to put on his good trousers when the mother called again: 'What the devil's father's keeping you?'

He went out as he was, walking with a sideways movement to conceal the big overcoat button that his inconsiderate mother had sewed on the fork of his trousers. He had never met this girl when he was at his best; there was always something to humble him – cow, coming from the bull, unshaven, or this big button.

She held the bicycle while he did the pumping and as he was stooped his head was against her beautiful bare legs. She spoke to him and this gave him a chance to upturn his eyes, but as an act of self-denial, a form of inverted bravado, he kept his eyes on the road. He felt that wearing those trousers any advance would be a waste of time and would maybe spoil a better future chance. He was fond of saving up for a grand passion.

Returning to the house he changed his trousers in the hope of

123

meeting the girl on her way back. It happened that while waiting in the bushes near the mouth of the road, Molly came up.

His problem now was whether to enjoy – as far as he would be allowed – the pleasures afforded by this slut or wait on for Mary. He decided that he might easily kill two birds with one stone. If Molly turned out a failure or even if she proved a success, he would still be able to meet the other girl.

He walked with her to the green road and chanced his arm with a few lewd double-meaning remarks as he had heard Charlie doing, never imagining that, as he so indifferently said them, they would have any effect.

They were beginning to work. Instead of being insulted, she laughed, and pretending that she had not caught one phrase – the hottest one – said: 'What was that you said?'

With lewd delight he repeated the phrase.

She kept silent waiting to hear more. He tried something the worst he could think of and again she took it in with a sigh. He found himself saying the most abominable things with a cold detachment; it was all in the cause of truth.

'Some of the blacks have ones a foot and a half.'

She sighed deeply again. They were treading their way through the nettles and stunted blackthorns.

Why hadn't he tried this method before?

They fell on a bank among the thistles and briars and all of a sudden his conscience returned. He was ashamed of himself and ashamed of being seen in Molly's company. She had large buck teeth and her eye teeth, unable to find space, were turned in like the teeth of a pike. The grass around was withered and nearby somebody had used the spot as a lavatory. In disgust he got to his feet.

'You wait a second here,' he said. He crossed the bank into Kerley's field, looked furtively round to make sure no one was watching or the girl following, and then he ran full speed through the field, indifferent to the bull sniffing in a corner, and was out on the main road in half a minute.

He hoped that no one had seen him – no one that mattered – but he was finding it hard to convince himself, for nothing could get it out of his head that as he was racing down the field Mary had been passing home on her bicycle. It would be just his luck if she saw him. The hedge was thick along the road at this point and it was doubtful if one passing on a bicycle could see him, but women, he always heard, had very sharp sight when it came to seeing things like that. Good God! wasn't he the fool to risk everything for – nothing.

Some time later when he had quietened his thoughts he decided to take a stroll towards the cross-roads – just to see.

Before he had come within speaking distance of the cross-roads he could see – or he thought he could see – jeering grins on several faces. He tried to hide his self-consciousness as he approached. He felt that every eye was on him. He put on a sour face and concentrated on high philosophical thoughts. He began to count the stones in the wall as an exercise in self-control.

There were, he observed, the usual two groups at the cross-roads – a main party discussing football, politics and the crops, and a fringe party of whom Charlie was the leader carrying on low lewd conversation or making insulting comments on the passers-by. This fringe had been having a competition as to which of them could shout the loudest and their bawling could be heard echoing in the valleys beyond the Parochial House and the river.

Tarry had tried to join the group under cover of this shouting but Charlie, in Tarry's egotistical view, seemed to have but one interest in life, and that was concentrating his nasty mind on Tarry. Charlie was quite decent when there was no third party present, but in a crowd he showed very nasty traits.

All Tarry wanted now was to join the crowd quietly, anonymously.

Among those present were the brothers Finnegan, Larry and Joe, sitting together on the edge of the bank.

'Did you get it?' said Charlie with a laugh, as Tarry came to a stop in the middle of the group of crooked old men who were debating the mighty feats of strength of their immediate forbears and in particular of a noted strong man known as Paddy Hughie Tom who had hurled the sixteen pound shot 'from here to below the turn at McKenna's gate'.

125

Tarry ignored Charlie's remark and tried to merge himself in the debating group by expressing a scientific view of Paddy Hughie Tom's throw.

'The world's record's well over fifty feet, but that would be well over the record. Was it the right weight or did he throw it right?'

A fellow with a long upper lip and bandy legs who was a relation of the strong man, spat out viciously and said: 'Throw it right! what the hell are you trying to come at?'

Tarry regretted having made the observation. Attention was being focused on him, the very thing he didn't want. The Finnegans were only waiting for the chance to pick a row.

'I'm sure he threw it that far,' he said, glancing down the hill towards McKenna's gate. 'He must have been a damn good man.'

'He was six feet four and built according,' remarked another.

'Don't be making a child of yourself, Tom,' said someone else. 'Did you ever see that man stripped? Chest on him, be the holies, like a barrel. Flynn,' the man turned to Tarry, 'did you say that the weight wasn't the right weight? Do you know what, he'd throw the breed of you over that bleddy ditch before his breakfast.'

Tarry tried to sidle away, to make himself invisible, but the argument was beginning to surge around him.

'He never tried to grab anyone's piece of land,' one of the Finnegans said from his sitting position.

'Huh,' sniffed Tarry with contempt. 'Grabbing land! That's a thing of the past.'

'Here's where Paddy Hughie Tom stood,' one of the crooked little hero-worshippers was saying. 'I was here the evening he did it.'

Two girls passed on bicycles.

'Me hand on your drawers,' shouted Charlie. 'Come back outa that, Flynn,' he said in a camouflaged voice, like the voice of a stunted mongrel bull.

'That's bleddy mean,' said Tarry weakly.

'He never grabbed what never belonged to him anyway,' jawed Larry Finnegan, who had got to his feet.

A man passed on a bicycle and someone called after him: 'You're going the wrong way.'

Immediately the man dismounted, and there was consternation when it was discovered that he was Father Markey. He stood at a distance of about thirty yards from the crowd listening to the breathing of the men, for the crowd was hushed as soon as his identity became known. After a minute or so he got on his bicycle again. If he had said something they would not have been half so disturbed. There would be more trouble over this, and nothing was more certain than that Tarry would be blamed more than anyone else.

Below them in the hollow the river gurgled by on the shiny stones. The mackerel sky was darkening.

'Are you sure it was him?' a man asked another.

'Absolutely.'

Eusebius arrived at this point and stood in the middle of the road leaning contentedly over the handle-bars of his bicycle. How easily he blended with this crowd, thought Tarry. He was one of them, not a disturbing influence as Tarry was.

'I'll make some of them hop,' growled Joe Finnegan. 'I'll bring some of them to their milk before I'm finished.'

Tarry, knowing that these remarks were directed towards him, and realizing that the night was coming on, thought it best to move off. As he was about to go he turned to Eusebius and asked him if he were coming.

'What the hell hurry's on you?' said Eusebius.

'I'm expecting a cow to calve.'

'She'll take no hurt.'

'Better be sure than sorry, Eusebius.'

'Any cow will calve on her own.'

From the mouth of the Drumnay road was heard the wild passionate neighing of a mare, and Eusebius jumped on his bicycle. It was a mare being brought to his stallion.

Nothing vexed Tarry more than this. To see how interested Eusebius could be in his own affairs and at the same time trying to make Tarry indifferent to *his*. It was a mean sort of attitude.

Joe Finnegan, afraid that Tarry might escape before he engineered a row with him, staggered across the bank and stumbled over Tarry's feet.

'Did you try to work the boot on me, Flynn?' he cried. 'The bastard tried to work the boot on me.'

The men who had been discussing Paddy Hughie Tom immediately came to attention. The one form of fighting which was abhorred in this society was the use of the boot in a row. The knee in the belly was permitted, but never the boot.

'I didn't even see the man atself,' pleaded Tarry.

'You're a liar,' bawled Larry Finnegan, surging up towards him.

'I'd bore rat-holes in you, and in the breed of you,' declared Joe.

Tarry moved away pursued by the Finnegans.

He decided to run, and he ran followed by the two brothers. He outdistanced them easily, but in doing so he had lost caste, he knew. When he stopped to draw his breath he could hear Joe laughing: 'He wouldn't be able to pull the skin of boiled buttermilk.'

As he walked up the Drumnay road among the gossiping poplars he had a feeling that there was some tension in his home. There was a light in the dairy window and although there was often a light in the dairy he sensed something wrong. Was it his guilty conscience?

The cow must have calved. Nervous activity registered itself from the vicinity of the cow house. The front door of the dwelling-house was open and that was a sure sign. He ran in and found the kitchen empty. The kettle was on the crook. He called hello but no one answered. Then his mother's footsteps crossed the street in front of the house and she saw him.

'Oh,' said she bitterly, 'it's you that's the good son. That the cow had like to be lost in the calving with not a man about the place. Only for the good neighbours I don't know what I'd do.'

He took his chastisement without a reply. He went to the door of the cow house and looked in with humble eyes. Paddy Callan and Petey Meegan were sitting together on the manger-stick smoking and talking and feeling that they were the two most important men in the parish. The cow lay contentedly beside them.

'Where's the calf?' he asked.

'He's here,' called Aggie from the horse stable, 'and come in and give us a hand to dry him.'

'A bull calf,' he remarked when he saw the little animal.

'That's why she got it so hard to calve – big head,' said Aggie complainingly.

'Nonsense. That cow always calved on her own. Almost any cow will calve on her own,' he added. 'And there's no need to be rubbing a calf in summer. And what half-chewed eejut brought the cow in from the field anyway in the middle of summer to the dirty stable?'

In the task of delivering a cow or any other farm animal the last men Tarry would have would be the pair of awkward fellows who were now sitting on the manger-stick. They took on to know a great deal and were fond of interfering with nature taking her course. Pawing the cow and rooting around her, there was a danger that she'd get blood poison from this handling.

'Leave the calf alone and he'll be on his feet in a minute,' Tarry said. 'That rubbing him with a wisp of grass is not needed.'

'Give that man no heed,' commanded the mother coming in.

'I was only . . .' He cut himself off lest his mother should go into the tantrums, and went to the cow house to have another look at the cow.

The road gate rattled and the mother looked to see who it was. It was the two daughters. 'Wet the tay,' she called, 'and fill up the tay-pot.'

The two old men were reminiscing about the past – Petey especially was – and Paddy as soon as he had an audience changed his attitude and began to take a hand at Petey – about his not having a wife – 'and all to that.'

Remembering Petey's attempted mimicry of him in Joe Finnegan's, Tarry was not over sympathetic. If Petey got the chance he could take a hand at a bigger fool than himself.

'There's your woman there,' laughed Paddy, putting his hand on Mary's shoulder when she was pouring out the tea. He winked at the girl. 'What do you say?'

Mary took it in good part and as for Petey he had the old bachelor's enjoyment in being joked about women. Petey ate away, scooping his egg out of the shell with the wrong end of a table spoon.

The mother sat in her usual place on the low stool by the fire quietly directing the conversation, but for the moment letting it run on the marriage business, saying nothing.

'Mam,' said Paddy turning half round, 'this will be the dearest cow that ever calved about your place. You'll lose one of your daughters over it. By the lord Harry there's a man there and wouldn't anyone know he has the heat of marriage in him.'

Observing Petey's reactions, so contented having his back scratched, Tarry felt embarrassed, but he tried to hide his feelings. He wasn't going to have his mother blaming him this time.

'Mary, run out and see if that cow is all right. I don't want her to eat her cleanings,' said the mother. 'Paddy, if she wants to get married the devil the bit of me will stop her.'

'Now Petey, it's up to you,' said Paddy.

Petey, his ego being built up, was inclined to retreat, to make himself more valuable.

'Before the girl comes in, what do you say, Petey?' Paddy urged.

'If I had me hay cut,' said Petey with a hem and a haw, 'and the house done up a bit, I don't know a damn but I might take a notion.'

'Ah now, none of this hunker-sliding, Petey,' said Paddy half on the joke. 'If you don't do it now you'll never do it. Damn it, after all it's coming up to the time for you to be making a move. I'm not saying you're past yourself yet, but at the same time it's coming up to the time.'

Tarry dragged an old newspaper from the window stool and began to pore over the advertisements. He was finding it hard to endure this embarrassing conversation.

Paddy turned to the mother. 'You wouldn't send her out empty-handed, Mary?'

'If she was getting a good man she'd be well treated,' said the mother.

'Now Petey,' said smiling Paddy.

'I wouldn't – I wouldn't think – much,' said Petey hesitantly.

Paddy was disgusted. He switched the conversation sharply, much to Petey's disappointment, and said: 'Are yous taking seed of your hay, Mary?'

'This man here says that there's no seed on it,' said the mother.

'Anayther there is,' said Tarry.

Mary returned. Petey glanced maukishly at her as if trying to make up his mind. Perhaps he sensed that in the long run the whole thing was a joke, that when it would come to the test the girl would reject him. Perhaps he didn't want to be hurt and that was the cause of his hesitation.

'We're as well be mooching off,' said Paddy rising.

'Musha what's your hurry?' said the mother looking at the clock. 'It's only half eleven; that clock's fast.'

'Time for any dacent man to be shunting, Mary.'

The men rose. The mother went to the dresser and took two half crowns out of an egg cup. Going out the door she slipped them into Paddy's hand. Tarry thought her very generous, more generous than she ever was with him, and he grumbled when the men were gone.

'It pays to be dacent,' said the mother. 'A shut fist never caught a bird. If you had your way we wouldn't have a neighbour to bid us the time of day. You'd smoke the tail of an ass and not a word about it. Aggie, go out and bring in the vessel.'

They sat up by the fire holding an inquest on the late discussion. 'That man's no good,' said the mother referring to Petey. '*He'll* never take a wife, never, never, never.'

'And who the hell said I'd take him?' snapped Mary. 'I wouldn't take him if his bottom was paved with diamonds.'

'And what do you mane to do? Yous all can't hang around this place. You might be glad of him yet.'

'Cod,' said Mary.

'Oh, yous are all like this man here, no sense or reason with any of yous.'

Tarry, sick of the whole thing, got up to go to bed. The mother said: 'Take up them pair of trousers that's hanging behind the door that I patched for you.'

Looking at the pair of old trousers with patches like deal planks all over them Tarry burst out: 'What in the Name of God do you want me to wear them oul' trousers for? To hell with them.'

The mother was ready to overflow in a rage. Tarry took the trousers. The mother said: 'Young Paddy Reilly was here this evening after you were gone and he wants to know if you'd go up the morrow and give them a hand with the spraying of the praties on the high hill where they can't work the horse sprayer. I said you'd go. And don't be making a fool of yourself up there the morrow.'

Tarry's heart gasped. To think of his having to go in those patched trousers to help in the spraying of Reilly's potatoes was the last irony. His mother could design the most degrading jobs for him. If it had been making hay atself, but spraying potatoes and going up and down the drills with clay on his boots and the old ragged trousers, worse even than the pair with the big button on the fork. The fork of this pair looked as if they had been torn by mad dogs and patched by mad women.

He took the trousers in his hand and went up to bed, and as he lay awake he tried to imagine himself as a great poet. He had written one poem for Mary which he liked and he said it over in his head, while in his imagination the girl was standing before him listening to poetry with all the innocent enthusiasm of the convent-bred girl who never fathomed the design behind it.

You do not come down the road any more
Past the ash trees where the gap in the hedge revealed
Your blue dress the trimming to the bottom of Callan's field.
And the free-wheel of your bicycle like the whirr
Of the breeze in the black sallies. If you could see
The clay of time falling away from my feet
When you appeared this side of Callan's gate,
You'd come.

He couldn't get a good last line and he abandoned the day-dream altogether. He imagined the girl again and this time he recited another poem – as his own.

Oh I'd wed you without herds, without money or rich array
And I'd wed you on a dewy morning at day dawn grey.

She fell into his arms and he fell asleep.

'Get up, you lazy loorpan, you.'

It was morning. After his day-dreams and night-dreams he awoke to the dreadful reality, the shame and degradation of the patchy trousers, and he himself no more than one of Reilly's servant boys.

He got out of bed, stooped to look out the window through the trees and though the sky looked cloudy he knew it would stay fine: it always did when he was wishing it to rain.

The mother was up. She wanted him to hurry on that he'd get his breakfast in Reilly's – 'and what's the use going to a man for a half-day? The gassan said that they'd send a man to you when you'd be drawing in the hay. And a day with the horse and cart is not to be sneezed at.'

Tarry delayed. He took his breakfast before going. At least he would be spared the ignominy of going in red-raw to Reilly's at that hour of the morning. He would have to trust to luck at dinner time, and even if the girl were in then he might not care so much when he got into the hang of the place.

'The book under the coat!' exclaimed the mother as he went out the door.

He turned and said: 'I have no book. What book do you mean?'

'Ach, ach. – And if you happen to meet one of these Finnegans up the road don't say one word. Last Saturday when I was at me confession I mentioned the trouble to Father Markey and he said them and Christians differ and that he was going to talk to them one of these days. There's not one of the priests that wouldn't put their hands under me feet. But you haven't the wit of a two-year-old child, always trying to belittle the people that 'id do you

133

a good turn. You're on the right side of Father Markey's book now and keep so.'

This kind of talk was better than anything to drive Tarry towards the day's disagreeable work, and he hurried out of his mother's range as quickly as he could. Nature must be like men in their loves – She likes to be resisted, not loved too easily.

Because Tarry was not interested in the beauty that was fluttering around him the more did the leaves dance and take on the simpleness that is so weird, and the more were the little hills queer with an ancient roguery. He did not love nature's works, but he was *in love* with them – and he wished he wasn't, for these things always made him sad, reminding of something far and forgotten in the land of Childhood before the Fall of Man.

He was impatient with the flirtatious gambolling of birds and trees, thinking as he was on the day ahead. But if he did not look at the hedges or the dust of the road these things looked at him.

Now he was caught in the stare of a huge boulder of whinstone that stood half way up the pass to Callan's house. The old people used to say that there were fairies under that stone which was one of the shoulder-stones hurled by Finn McCoole, and Tarry knew that there were fairies under it – real fairies, fairies of the imagination, bitter and ironic fairies too.

There had been several heaps of similar boulders in Eusebius' fields which were even more fairy-invested but Eusebius had cleared them all away. Tarry agreed with him in one way, for he too was ruthless, but at the same time he was beginning to think that Paddy Callan was a wiser man in the long run, though Paddy himself denied that he believed in the fairies and said that the only reason he didn't shift the boulder was its usefulness as a scratching post for the cattle.

The green bushes at the bend beyond Callan's gate overhung the road and the place in the dewy morning was a strange land in which a man could adventure. Going round this bend he always expected to meet someone or something strange. He let down his braces so as to give a devil-may-care appearance to the trousers. If a man could give the impression that he enjoyed wearing such patched things it would make them look funny.

134

It was his experience that women liked a man who was queer and funny and didn't care for anything. In this way the trousers were even worse looking. The fork hung down like the udder of a cow and the waist gave the impression that the wearer had a big belly. He tightened the braces again. He hurried past Cassidy's house and cut across the bottom of Cassidy's long meadow in case he might run into Joe Finnegan near the mouth of his lane. He looked across at Carlin's and his new place and got a thrill out of the ownership. He was so glad to see that the four ash trees on the near fence were still standing. He stood on the edge of a ditch to see if he could see his cattle, though his mother had told him that in future one of the girls would keep an eye on them till the other trouble blew over.

Nobody was up in Carlin's. He could hear the crow of the old cock in the stable and his knowledgeable mind reflected on the foolishness of the Carlins in keeping an old cock. Nothing but in-bred fowl about that place.

The memory of the night before flashed through his mind and he did not think it funny. He was disgusted with the attitude of his mother to an old man like Petey, and at her suggestion that she'd be prepared to give money with Mary if the marriage took place.

What was that? He listened and was almost certain that the cries came from Finnegan's; the man was beating his wife.

When he arrived at Reilly's potato field it looked as if the men had been at work for a long time. Three men with knapsack sprayers on their backs were climbing the steep hill before the house. The head of the household, a small wizened fellow, was rushing about the headland wearing a peculiar grin of authority, the joking face of a slave-driver.

'Hah,' he squealed, 'where were you before dinner?'

One would think he was paying me, thought Tarry as he tried to joke back. Another sprayer, which happened to be a leaky one, was put on Tarry's back. The old man stood at the barrel and filled it quickly with a small tin can. 'Off you go now, don't say it was here you were kept,' said he.

Bored and miserable he climbed the hill, doing his best to

135

dream himself far away, famous, and all this world in its proper place.

At dinner as he sat at the long deal table among six men who ate with their knives and belched and smacked, he kept his eyes on the plate self-consciously and sipped from the mug of buttermilk without tilting his lips.

The girl, helped by her mother and a servant girl, served the food. She shoved the dishes of potatoes on to the table between himself and her brother and as she did so she rubbed against his shoulder.

He would never be able to recover from this day's shame.

Going home that evening with his heart in the gutter he met the girl and from her attitude he believed that she did not mind his ragged clothes or the fact that he was one of the working men. She could see through the appearances to the reality.

He was tempted.

He knew that ladies had often fallen in love with their workmen. He could well have a happy time with the girl if he could bring himself to accept that point of view. But it was impossible.

A man who has conquered can dictate his own terms, but this would be slavery.

What the girl said to him he hardly knew. He was listening to his own divided self raising a bedlam in his imagination.

He knew that he had insulted her.

'Will you be at the dance on Sunday night?' she asked.

'Dancing is an eejut's game,' he said. And he went on to expatiate on the folly of dancing. 'What would you say to a bunch of horses that after a hard day's work spent the night galloping and careering round the field? I wouldn't *dream* of wasting me time at a dance.'

'I'd love you to come,' she said sweetly.

'I wouldn't bother me bleddy head,' he said with a loud laugh.

'Still – ' She gave him a gentle smile but he was determined.

'It's only an eejut's game.'

'Sunday night will be a big event, Tarry. I could see you there.'

'Indeed you couldn't and don't be pretending you could,' he shouted. He kept in a twist to conceal as much of his patched clothes as possible.

'You'll probably be there all the same,' she said.

'I wouldn't be seen dead at that hall.'

... My God! my God! my God! he cried in his heart when they had parted. He knew that he had meant nothing of what he had said. It was all the bravado of a man in ragged clothes.

He wanted to fling himself prostrate on the ground and ask the earth's forgiveness for his stupidity. He talked to himself. He rehearsed the encounter in his mind and said the right things. He was soft. He let the girl mould him. And then the raw reality appeared through the day-dream and he cried again.

What is the matter with me? Why couldn't I say the right things?

He glanced back and the setting sun was shining on the back windows of the house. Silly sun to think that I could be comforted by your illusory gold.

' – hell light down on you and that's my prayer.'

'And me dead tired!'

The mother had been waiting at the gate.

'Oh, it's you that's the darling boy,' she cried.

'What's wrong now?'

'What's wrong! Oh, I don't know what class of a man you are.'

'Can't you tell me what's wrong and not be making a mystery of it?'

'Go on in there and put on a dry pair of trousers and a clean shirt and I'll tell you.'

'Tell me first.'

'Go in and change your wet dirty clothes or will you drive me clane and dacent out of me mind ... Ah ha, good evening, Paddy ...'

Tarry went in to change his clothes. Shortly afterwards the mother came in.

'Had you a hard day?'

'I put on four barrels with a leaky sprayer and that was no joke climbing one of them hills,' he said appealing for pity. 'What were you talking about outside?'

'Aggie, put on the kettle and make tay for this man.'

The mother kept him in suspense. She discussed practically everything about the place in spite of all his attempts to get her to unfold the mystery. When he had his tea taken and everything had been discussed she said in a low voice: 'What carry-on had yous at the cross the other evening?'

Tarry showed blank innocence.

'You attacked the priest,' she declared in an awful whisper.

'What would take a priest up at the cross?'

'Oh, this is more of it. Just when I was getting well in with the priests you had to attack the poor priest. And then ran.'

'I don't know what you're talking about.'

'Well, he's coming up again in the morning and I hope you'll have a good excuse for him. – That there's nobody like you. Aye, indeed,' she sighed. 'Will you take a look at that letter we've got from Daly, the solicitor, this morning? It's there on the dresser.'

He looked at the letter and made slighting comments on its literary style.

'Illiterate.'

'I suppose,' said the mother, 'you could write as good a letter as a solicitor – or a schoolmaster.'

'That wouldn't be hard,' said Tarry with a sneer.

'O, Lord, O Lord! If ever a man would make a person throw off their guts it's you. The Lord have mercy on your father but that *was* the man to state a letter. If he was alive I wouldn't have to be sending these ones to the town to see the attorney.'

'To see the attorney. This letter only says that he'd like to see one of us whenever we happened to be in the town. There doesn't appear to be any hurry about us going, as far as I can see.'

'And why is it that we haven't the deed complete by this? If I could depend on you I wouldn't care, but I can't trust you as far as I'd throw you. Mary should be back any time now.'

'So she went to the town to see him. Didn't I tell you that I'd

138

go out on the bike and see him. When I went the first time I should go the second time. What will he think?'

'And another thing,' said the mother now that she had her hand in, 'keep away from that slob of a Brady one. I do be hearing things about her – God protect everyone's rearing – and last Sunday Bridgie McArdle was telling me that she's a peculiar class of a girl. Charlie Trainor does be coming about Brady's house and I'd keep away if I was you.'

'And you always praising him.'

'Never you mind. Now that you have your tay taken and the fresh clothes on, you might run and meet Bridie with the milk. Keep away from that party. Be dangerous to throw a pair of trousers at some women.'

Standing in the doorway Tarry saw the three calves which had been in Carlin's in the meadow. 'Who took them calves down?' he asked.

'I had them brought down till things are settled about the curse o' God deed.'

'That's just giving in,' said he as he went to meet his sister.

When he returned, Mary had arrived from the town and was explaining to the mother what the solicitor had said. The mother bare-footed by the fire was sitting with her head on one side listening carefully.

'And you told him what I told you to say?'

'The whole bill of the races.'

Tarry wasn't being let into the secret at all. The mother was making a child of him, an irresponsible child – and all because he was able to see the wild and wonderful meaning in the commonest things of earth.

Could he not extract from this very trouble something wild and wonderful too? Was there not a second Tarry of whom nobody in Drumnay was aware, not even his mother, who looked on at the mortal Tarry, watching, laughing, criticizing and recording? He saw himself sitting there in the corner with his elbows on the table while his mother and sisters talked. Though he was silent his was the only opinion that would matter in the long run.

Out of this imagination of himself he suddenly emerged to declare:

'In a hundred years from now the only thing that will ever be remembered about this savage area is that I lived here awhile among the pigs.'

To attempt to describe the look on Mrs Flynn's face at this surprising outburst would be impossible. She showed in her countenance a mixture of terror and laughter. She stood the pot-stick up against the hob and said: 'Put out that dog till we say the Rosary. Give me over the wee stool till I kneel on it. With the help of God we'll both go out on the fair day and if yous can get that house well and good maybe it id be all for the best. A good eating-house is not to be laughed at. I suppose you mentioned the row this wonderful man here had with that savage, Joe.'

'I did,' said Mary.

As they were beginning the evening prayer Tarry saw his mother looking at him and he believed that she was impressed by his boast and the thought depressed him. It was a responsibility being depended upon, being considered a wise man. Bad as he was now he didn't want *that*.

> Thou O Lord wilt open my lips.
> And my tongue shall announce Thy praise.

'Did you put in your bike, Mary?'

7

He was 'hanging' a scythe in the kitchen the next morning to mow around the rocks and corners in the hay-field, when looking out the back window he saw the Parish Priest himself coming up the road. He was walking slowly and the hauteur of his sided head as he strode between the poplars took away some of the terror. He was making up his mind to have it out with Father Daly unknown to his mother, if he could keep her out of it. He felt that outside the destructive influence of his mother he could put himself over big with the priest. On an entirely new high level of literature and scholarship.

Whether his mother came on the scene or not that was the way he was going to talk. The more a man stuck to the gutter the more he was stuck in it and he was not going to be the wet gutter reflecting the sky of truth if he could help it. His mother was over in the potato field at the time and he had high hopes that she would not return till the priest had left. In this he was disappointed. Just then the dog – which was an irreligious beast – began to bark wildly from the haggard and in a moment he was galloping across the street in front of the door. The mother who was coming across the meadow on her way back from the field saw the dog and rushed ahead just in time to prevent the priest from being attacked by the mongrel.

Tarry was in the house screwing his courage to the sticking place and indifferent to the dog's behaviour.

'You're welcome, father. Chu father – dog.'

Father Daly had his hand on the bar of the gate. The woman was in a terrible state, shaking like jelly. The presence of the avowed and sacred celibate is a terror to womankind. No chink in the heart.

'Chu – father – dog – to hell – father.'

The priest kept his dignity and never relaxed the hauteur of his sided head. He seemed to be staring at the chimney of the house.

The woman succeeded in getting a kick at the dog, and this and the sound of Eusebius' cart coming down the road drew the animal away, for the dog had a warm regard for Eusebius, preferring him to his own master.

Having bid the woman the time of day Father Daly said: 'In the words of Shakespeare, Mrs Flynn:

> A little learning is a dangerous thing,
> Drink deep or taste not the Pierian spring.'

'Pope,' said Tarry under his breath, too low for the priest to hear, but loud enough to flatter his own ego.

'Yes, father,' whimpered the woman.

The cart approaching had stopped among the bushes and its stopping drew attention to its presence.

'Finnegan's cart,' remarked the priest.

'Or Eusebius',' said the mother.

'Finnegan's,' dogmatized the priest, who took a great delight in knowing ordinary things.

Neither mother nor son contradicted him. Tarry was pleased at the priest's attitude. He was going to argue on the higher plane and that suited Tarry perfectly. He was not so pleased when Father Daly said in a declamatory tone: 'This son of yours is a perfect fool, Mrs Flynn. A perfect fool. Yes, he takes on to know things that men have spent years in colleges to learn. Why don't you get him a wife? The other night, I understand he was at this cross-roads of Drumnay sowing the seeds of doubt in the minds of decent men.'

'But – ' Tarry was about to defend himself, but his mother standing one side of the priest gave him a look of mingled hate and pity that killed the spirit in him.

'Oh my God, father,' said the mother piteously.

'Yes, Mrs Flynn, talking about religion to fools, that is what we spend years in colleges for.'

During a pause in the priest's remarks the woman was able to get in a bit of flattery. 'I heard people to say, father, that out from the bishop you were the educatedest man in the diocese.'

142

Father Daly smiled. 'The bishop is a very great scholar, Mrs Flynn, a very great scholar. You'll be doing a fine job for God and Ireland, Mrs Flynn, if you get this man married and settled down.'

'Isn't that what I'd like, father,' said she. 'But sure God help us I can't see much future for girls in this place at all. If the girls were married I'd be only too glad to see him bringing in a wife. None of the other marriageable men of this place believe in making a move at all. What do you make of them, father?'

Up against this problem of the decay of the will to continue the human species theology was helpless, and the priest changed the conversation sharply to the weather and the crops.

The woman was disappointed in the priest. She thought him as blind to the ways of the world as her son. She had wanted to raise the question of the Finnegans and the Carlins and other matters of political importance, but he was beyond such details.

'We're having some trouble with the Finnegans,' said she.

'Very hot tempered indeed,' said he casually.

Tarry sidled away and the woman and the priest began to discuss the fowl, a subject in which Father Daly took an interest.

Tarry listened from the doorway of the hen house, pretending to be examining the hinges of the door.

Eusebius was delaying up the road till the priest went away. Tarry took the scythe and went to the hay-field.

As he went off he could see the priest's face beam with pleasure. Father Daly liked to see a man going to do his day's work.

As far as he could now gather, his mother was trying to impress upon the priest the importance of getting the deed of the farm through as well as the lesser matters of keeping Joe Finnegan quiet and stirring the men to get married.

Death was in the atmosphere.

Only the yellow weeds in the meadow were excited by living.

That was May Callan now on her bicycle going off to work in the factory.

The next day Paddy Reilly sent a man with a pair of horses

143

and a mowing machine to cut Flynn's hay, that being the arrangement come to when Tarry helped at the spraying of Reilly's potatoes.

The day after that was the fair day and his mother and two sisters, Mary and Aggie, went to the town.

Bridie was in great humour at the idea of the other sisters leaving to start a restaurant in the town.

'That'll be the cooking that slept without,' said she.

He went to the hay-field to make the hay, making it up in windrows, where it was light on the heights. Tomorrow he would have his sisters to help him. The dry earth under his feet was slippery, but the mown hay was filled with memories of life. The scent of the wild woodbine in the hedge bedrugged his mind until he felt no worry. He was a very tiny creature in the middle of a large field.

Beyond the hedge was Brady's, but today nobody was about the house. He concluded that they had gone to the fair. Even if they were at home he was determined to have no more to do with Molly.

He watched the bright yellow frogs leaping about on the dry earth, and the insects that crawled in the ruts. He got down on his knees and began to study a beetle that lay on its back. For no reason at all but only because it existed and he existed.

The hoarse caw of hungry crows sounded from the plantations in the Whitestone Park.

The whole world was gone to the fair and he had it all to himself.

That day when he went home for his dinner he found a letter awaiting him on the dresser. The letter was from his uncle Petey, who to Tarry's knowledge had only written about twice in twenty-five years. He was then, according to the letter, with a circus in Tullamore – Ringmaster.

What would Mrs Flynn say if she heard about that? The uncle hinted that he might call if in the vicinity.

The mother and two daughters came home filled with excitement. They had rented a shop in the main street and were planning to have a restaurant going for the next fair day.

'Waiting for the bleddy geldings to make a move,' said the mother, 'is nothing but foolishness. An odd bag of praties or a few heads of cabbage and little things like that will put a bone in your business,' she said, the feeling of prosperity in her expression. 'No need for new-fangled cooking. Give the men their fill and that's all they want. Lord O! Come here.'

She was looking out the back window. Tarry went to help her to look. Eusebius was coming up the road driving a number of bullocks before him. 'One – two – three, four, five, six,' the mother counted. 'That's the man will make a spoon or spoil a horn. I must go out and have a talk with him to see how much he gave for them.'

Tarry followed her out, for he wanted to have a word with Eusebius too.

'Ah ha, it's you that's the right industrious boy that'll have a thing, not like this man of mine that I don't know what class of a sling-slang he is. You gave a brave penny for them, Eusebius.'

Eusebius let the cattle wander up the road and he continued talking with great enthusiasm when they broke into Callan's field of oats.

'How much do you think, Mary?'

'Did you give ten apiece, Eusebius?'

'I did and the rest, Mary.'

'And they're worth it. When they get a bit of grass they'll be wonderful animals, Eusebius. There's no doubt about it we're only in the ha'penny place with you, Eusebius. In the ha'penny place. You don't be at the curse-o'-God books, troth you do not – This man here – '

'We're only in the ha'penny place with *him*, Mary.'

There was a hardness about Eusebius' speech and behaviour this evening. He gave the idea of power and seemed to be losing his soft feminine way of going on.

'I'll see you later,' said he to Tarry who, when he got the opportunity, had a word in private with his neighbour. 'I'll be down the road in about an hour.'

'I wouldn't let them about me place,' said the mother later to her son, referring to Eusebius' cattle. She murmured to herself:

'Five of as hungry a cattle as ever I saw Must have bought them from some of the long-nosed scutch-grass farmers of Monaghan. Give us a hand off with this pot.' They shifted the pot. 'Why don't you take pattern by Eusebius?' said the mother. 'The song the blackbird sang to Paddy MacNamee is the truest song ever sung – "have it or do without it". These pair will be going to Shercock one of these days to start an eating-house and in no time you'd have a free house here. I think you'll have rain, for I have this corn on me wee toe and it's at me again. I wonder would you get the razor blade and pare it for me . . .

'Oh, that's the boy that'ill have a thing when we're all going hungry behind the hay. Mind now, don't draw the blood. I think, now, I put a sprag in the Finnegans' wheel over that law case. Between ourselves you could have worse neighbours. I'd rather them a damn sight than this sneaky Eusebius that you'd think butter wouldn't melt in his mouth. Oh, it's you that could have the good time here. You know I'm not too contented about that solicitor, though Father Daly said he'd see about it. O, please God it will come all right. You that could be the independent man . . .'

The mother brought the crocks up from the dairy and cleaned them in the kitchen so that she could enjoy the gossip with her son who was now, in her own words, 'coming to his milk'.

In a sing-song dreamy voice she began to build up a picture of his future for him.

'I wouldn't prevent you bringing in a woman here and I wouldn't be too stiff about money either. Sure there's not one in the parish cares less for money than I do or would more like to see you with your pockets full when you went out – so long as you wouldn't spend it.

'If the Lord spared us all you could have your nice pony and trap to bring us to Mass of a Sunday and devil than the beggars. I wouldn't have to be looking at them galloping past me the way they do. Mind you I wouldn't say a ha'porth to an odd little read of the books so long as you didn't make a male of them. This house will be empty shortly, these pair are going to Shercock next Wednesday – and in here again they'll never show their noses if

146

I can help it. Could keep a pair of horses and a pony all the year round ... I wonder what the devil's father them people wanted to know about the hen. The same inspectors have us polluted, if it's not the washing of the eggs, it's the bulls. There's a wee grain of rice there in the pot if you'd like it. Oh, it's you that could tell them all to kiss your arse.'

She carried the two crocks to the dairy with an air of deepest contentment, her talk wandering on towards the fulfilment of her dream as she groped about in the dairy.

Outside it was raining on the leaves of the lilac and the stones in the street glistened. The world that stretched east was so sorrowful this evening; and yet so beautiful.

If a man could only get his desire he could enjoy life and all the magic that was in common earth. But Tarry was a sensitive man, not a countryman, but merely a man living. And life was the same everywhere. He walked in a maze through the street, leaned over the bars of the road gate. He was always expecting something. Down that silent road something or someone different, not of this world, seemed to be about to come. That bend hid – what did it hide? His destiny, perhaps.

On the Thursday following he drove into Shercock with a load of new potatoes and other things for his sisters. The sisters left home the day before. The evening before they were due to leave Petey Meegan called and did his best to persuade them to stay. There was no future in an eating-house in a small town like Shercock that hadn't even a railway running to it.

Mary pointed out that there were the buses now. And anyhow she wouldn't stay if he was thirty years younger 'and that wouldn't be so very young.'

'Go home and buy yourself a blessed candle,' said she to him.

'I don't mind what you were up to this ...' he started to say but she cut him off.

'You poor fool, it's the Last Sacraments you ought to be thinking of. You and your fifty! You're not trusting to sixty.'

'It's a long road there's not a turn on,' said Petey going out the door with his tail between his legs.

'A short one there's not a cow-dung on,' retorted Mary.

'Thanks be to God,' she sighed when he had gone. 'I never felt in such good form.'

'I don't know so much about that,' said the mother.

'You know well,' said the girl, 'and it's not his age either, old as he is. There's something unnatural about that man. I heard Eusebius talking about his carry-on. I wouldn't like to eat the eggs his hens lay.'

Tarry, sitting on the load of meal, vegetables and new potatoes remembered that hint of Eusebius' and wondered what he meant.

Then he forgot as he turned at Drumnay cross-roads and the song of the axle changed to a low solemn hum on the dusty silent road.

It was the day after the market and the town was deserted. He delivered his load, bought the paper, a packet of cigarettes and three sweet buns. The sisters gave him tea.

He was bringing home two bags of cement and a couple of boards for the repair of the stables. In the hardware shop he met a man who said to him: 'I saw a friend of yours in Longford a week ago, an uncle of yours, I think.'

That uncle was coming nearer to his native place. Mrs Flynn would not be pleased.

Father Markey's car was standing outside the post office. The priest himself came out as Tarry was passing on his way home and Tarry tried to look as *decent* as possible. The priest was making preparations for the big concert and dance that was to be held in the hall the following Sunday night and in the quietness of his proud heart Tarry had dreams of being invited by Father Markey to take part. He felt that he would be able to rehabilitate himself with Mary Reilly if he once got the chance to flower forth in his real colours of genius. In spite of what he might pretend the priest was hardly blind to the fact that Tarry was well above the average man in ability. He could scarcely pass him over. The thing would be too obvious.

The priest gave him a quick glance as he entered his car and he did not seem too unfriendly.

In his conversations with Eusebius and his own mother he

passed the coming event over as a thing unworthy of his consideration. 'Just a bunch of poor ignorant people trying to amuse themselves,' was how he described it.

Privately he was dreaming, dreaming. This was a great cultural event and right into his barrow.

Sometimes he took an unholy pleasure in imagining that he had been passed over for one of the leading parts on the stage – it showed them all up as a crowd of ignoramuses. This self-pitying torture was too great to endure for long and he returned to his dreams. That had been going on for the previous two weeks since the news of the event had become warm. Day after day he had been expecting the curate's car to come up the road and the curate to ask him to get ready for the big role.

On the day that Father Daly had called he did himself fair justice, he thought. He had put himself well forward in the priest's good books. But as the big event approached and he was neither asked to take part nor was in possession of any inside information as to what was being planned, he had that awkward, embarrassing feeling that comes over a man when he finds that his talents are not indispensable to mankind. It seemed that the utterly ridiculous was about to happen – he not to be asked.

Saturday evening came. Meeting Eusebius – who, as far as he knew was in the same boat – he threw out a few hints about the concert in the hope that Eusebius would talk without realizing that Tarry was in the dark.

'I hear all the tickets are gone,' said Eusebius.

'What!' said Tarry.

'Did you not get one?'

'I wouldn't be seen dead at an affair of that kind. You didn't chance to hear who's going to be performing, Eusebius?'

'Don't you know, the usual – all the educated people, the three schoolmasters, the stationmaster and the postman that's what-you-might-call the right singer. You know you want a bit of education to go up on a stage,' Eusebius said without irony. He was quite sincere.

He said he heard that notable artistes had been booked from places as far distant as Castleblaney and Dundalk – and the band was coming all the way from Clones. Tarry was choked with grief and humiliation.

'Wouldn't you be as good on the stage as any of them?' he managed to say.

'Jabus now, sure wouldn't you be as good as me?'

Wasn't Eusebius the pitiful fellow, lacking any self-respect or regard for the inner qualities of a man. Tarry never breathed a word about his own ambitions, and all he could do as he went about his work that evening was to carry on the favourite and futile tradition of the Gaelic race – cursing the concert and the promoters of it. He wished that it might rain bucketfuls on the Sunday evening, and in his spiteful day-dream and ill-wish he saw two car-loads of the principal artistes in a fatal accident just outside the village. The accident would have to happen before the event so that they wouldn't have the pleasure of collecting the money. He hated Father Markey and he was determined to let the cat out of the bag as to his knowledge of the Church, and how it was not sound. He could ruin the Faith in that parish.

Eusebius hadn't told his companion everything, for the next evening when Tarry went down to the village, in the last forlorn hope that before it was too late the curate, the police, the school-masters and the stationmaster might see the light and realize the laughing-stock they were making of themselves, he found that Eusebius had been offered a job at the concert – carrying water from the pump to make tea for the visitors, and making himself generally useful. Eusebius had scarcely an eye for Tarry as he hurried to the pump beside the graveyard for 'water for the tay for the swanks'.

'And why the hell didn't you tell a fella? you're too bleddy mean.'

Eusebius laid down his two cans of water with the conscious-ness of the honour which had been conferred upon him and slowly lit a cigarette.

'Didn't I tell you that Father Markey asked me three weeks ago, the day I was coming from the mill? You could be on this job if you had to mention it to me at the time.'

'Who the hell said I wanted the job?'

'There you are now,' said Eusebius very independently and picked up his cans.

Eusebius so proud pushed his way through the crowd that was rushing to and fro around the door trying to get in. The hall was packed. John Magan with his palms upraised came to the door and appealed to the crowd to go home 'like good Catholics and go to bed'.

Tarry stood on the edge of the crowd and was pushed about more than most because he had his eyes on the vision of himself as he ought to have been – up on the stage reciting *The Outlaw of Loch Leine*.

Cars pulled up and men and women tremendous with airs of self-confidence. Car doors were banged, women were escorted by their men companions and they swept through the crowd around the door with a dominating flourish.

Through the open windows of the concrete hall the blare of the latest dance tunes came and the crooked little men, small farmers, standing in knots on the roadway chewing tobacco declared that the music was 'damn good'.

'And why wouldn't it and it after coming from Clones? Every man jack of that band gets a pound and a kick for his night.'

'A week's wages,' said someone else. 'Easy earned money.'

Tarry wanted much to go home but the old weakness which held him to the place of the insult kept him there waiting for kicks. He was hoping to be able to see Eusebius who might be able to get him a free pass in or even a ticket for money; so desperate was he at this moment that he would only be too glad to pay the half crown entrance.

Everybody that was anybody appeared to be coming that evening. The publican's wife, splay-footed, made her way through the throng at the door, the stationmaster and all his family came, there was a member of the County Council and others of fame. Tarry's ego receded till he could scarcely feel it at all.

A group of the village boys were groping along the hall trying to get a look in the windows and Tarry was tempted to join them. If he could get one look in he would be satisfied.

A sudden silence fell upon the rowdy crowd and Tarry, looking

151

round, found Father Markey pushing his way towards the door, carrying in his hand a valise. With him was the village schoolmaster's son and – Mary Reilly.

Tarry stood in to avoid being seen.

Now, thought he, I must get in at all costs. What was keeping that Eusebius? He couldn't but know the predicament Tarry was in. Tarry walked along the sidewall of the hall in utterest misery. He was uneasy too at the presence in the tobacco-chewing crowd of Larry Finnegan. Larry had been standing at the back of the crowd against the wall as still as a post but taking everything in. Tarry sensed danger. In the porch the priest and some other men were counting the money taken at the door.

'Be a great stunt to rob him,' someone remarked.

'Must have made thirty-five quid.'

Another car-load pulled up and emptied itself out. It appeared that some member of this car-load made a complaint when he got into the hall, for the curate came out and ordered the crowd to disperse at once. The crowd shivered a little and retreated a few yards but when the priest went back to count the rest of the money everyone had moved forward again. Next thing was someone at the back flung Tarry's cap into the porch. Tarry had a notion that it was Larry Finnegan but he pretended not to know, not wanting to raise a row. He went after his cap and as he did so the crowd surged forward and he was driven into the porch right into the small of Father Markey's back. The priest jumped up and Tarry tried to escape, but was jammed in a corner.

'You're the cause of all the trouble,' declared the priest, catching him by the shoulder.

Tarry saw at a glance that all the respectable eyes in the vicinity of the door inside the hall were upon him, and every eye said the same thing: 'Who is the half-wit?'

He was thrown out without ceremony to the loud laughter of the crowd outside. But home he would not go. Worse than this could not happen to him.

Two men from the nearest town whom Tarry knew crossed the road on their way to the hall to perform; they were dressed as Laurel and Hardy.

Within the hall he could now hear the start of what he had most hoped to take part in – the Question Time. Nobody in that hall would have had a look in with him in a competition of this kind and yet here he was cast out into exterior darkness. Again the curate appeared in the doorway of the hall. He said: 'Anybody outside who hasn't a ticket must go away at once. Anyone who isn't away within five minutes will be forcibly driven off by the police.'

Old men nudged one another and said: 'Are you coming?'

'I suppose we're better.'

The crowd dribbled away and Tarry was left by himself waiting there in the hope that his companion would yet appear. The priest saw him and came out. 'What are you doing here?' he snarled. 'Did I not tell you to get away?'

'I'm waiting for somebody, father,' he pleaded.

'Flynn, I'm giving you another minute to make yourself scarce.'

A group of oily-haired young men, shop-boys and cattle-dealers and factory workers lounged in the doorway smoking and observing the peasant being shoved around.

How Tarry vowed destruction to society on that occasion. He would have struck the priest if he didn't know that to do so would be as good as committing suicide; those slick townsmen would pounce upon him in a flash.

'Hook it, now,' said the priest.

'Don't push me, I am going.'

'Well, keep going, keep going.'

He moved away towards the village and as he did he could hear the giggle of the priest and the young men in the doorway.

'Who is he?' one asked, and the priest said: 'He's an idiot called Flynn.' There was more laughter at this and then the group in the doorway went inside.

At the corner of the public house many of the crowd who had been lounging around the hall waited. Tarry was too depressed to join them. He decided to return to the hall just for once. He might see Eusebius or some of the others who would be coming out for a mouthful of fresh air.

As luck would have it he ran into Eusebius on his way to the pump for more water.

'God, these swanks drink the devil's amount of tay,' said Eusebius. 'Do you know what' said he when he found that Tarry did not appreciate his joke, 'I'm looking for you all night. Where did you go?'

'Who's inside?' asked Tarry in desperation.

'All the boys, all the boys.'

'But what women?'

'The usual. Have a fag.'

'No. Wait till I hear.'

'Take one of these cans and you can snaffle your way in.'

'I wouldn't chance it. Father Markey's there and he'd only go for me.'

'He'll be going off with the money shortly and you can get in when he's away.'

This was as good a proposition as any. But the priest would be coming back as soon as he had left the money safely in the Parochial House, and that would only take him ten minutes in the car. 'Give me one of them cans, Eusebius.'

Going up to the door of the hall Tarry was elated and he was filled with goodwill towards Eusebius.

They left the cans of water in the little room off the doorway where a number of the local women, Molly included, were cooking for the artistes and stewards. It was impossible to get past the crowd that jammed the doorway so Tarry had to be content with a perch at the back among the old men.

The concert was coming to an end by this time. Two little girls were tap dancing as the dancers danced on the films. In his happier moments Tarry would have been inclined to think this form of step-dancing vulgar, but so pleased was he to have got in at all that he thought it the most delightful entertainment.

He was settling down to enjoy himself and was putting his ego together again when the schoolmaster's son got up on the stage and announced that the next item on the programme would be a song by Mr Christopher accompanied on the piano by Miss Mary Reilly.

Does your mother come from Ireland?
Sure there's something in you Irish . . .

There was a patriotic hush as Father Markey's brother ren-
dered this song, everyone except Tarry thinking it patriotic in the
extreme. Tarry had to hide his critical thoughts and look happy
when the man sang as an encore:

The hills of Donegal
To me you ever call
In every wind that wanders o'er
The wide and lonesome sea . . .

In the loud applause that followed Tarry did not hear the
voice of Father Markey as he returned. He inquired if anyone
had rushed the door in his absence or if they had had any trouble.
The answer being no he went into the cooking department and
was loud in laughing conversation with the women in no time.

The next announcement was that the hall had to be cleared for
the dance and that only those with the special green tickets
could regain admission without paying an extra half crown.

Tarry hurriedly searched his pockets. He had only two shillings
and twopence. He would be only too glad to pay this sum to get
to the dance though he didn't dance, for he wanted to see how
the affair would end and he had a particular interest in one girl
present.

But where would he get the extra fourpence? Fourpence
wasn't much when a man had it but when he hadn't twopence
was as hard to get as two pounds. How would he ask for it and
whom? The men on the door might take the two and two and
they might decide to make a show of him; and if Father Markey
was there he would be sure to make a show of him and tell him
to go home and frame his two and twopence.

Charlie Trainor going out in a gabble of conversation was too
busy to stop. A man like Charlie, it seemed to Tarry, could tell
by instinct when a man was trying to borrow him. He could
ask his sister Bridie only he wouldn't give her the gratification.
She wouldn't wait till morning to tell the mother about his
'begging'.

He found Eusebius. 'Eusebius, I wonder could you lend us fourpence till the morrow.' Tarry laughed as he said this just to show the ridiculosity of his asking such a small sum.

Eusebius hadn't a penny on him. He gave the last ha'penny he had for a packet of fags before he came in.

'Throw them the two and two, it's good enough for them.'

'Only give them the chance to laugh at me.'

'If I had it you'd get it, Tarry, you know that.'

'Oh, I know that,' said Tarry bitterly.

He watched the crowds re-enter for the dance and listened carefully to hear if any of the 'hard chaws' of the place would try to make a bargain at the door as he often heard them doing. But on this occasion every man of them shelled out his half crown as if he were only too glad to do so.

It was clear to Tarry, and the priest was standing in the porch talking to the doorman, that if he tried to get in for the two and two he would only create a scene. So he made up his mind to wait outside and pick up as much of the pleasurable emotion of the dance as filtered through the windows and door. He would be satisfied now if the priest left him alone.

The dance was in full swing now.

Couples began to drift out and make for the graveyard. Among these he was almost certain he noticed Charlie and Molly. He had a mind to follow them and find out for sure, but at that moment Father Markey wandered out to the middle of the road and looked up and down, so Tarry stood in the shadow of the hedge and lay low. Some time later Eusebius came out for two more cans of water and Tarry ran out eagerly to speak to him.

'How is it going on, Eusebius?'

'A few nice bulling heifers in there, right enough.'

'Who's Mary Reilly dancing with?'

Eusebius considered for a moment and then thought that as far as he could remember she wasn't there at all. 'I don't think she waited for the dance. Why?'

'Oh, nothing.'

'A lot of the swanks didn't wait, you know.'

'If I had that extra fourpence ...'

'Hardly worth your while now.'

It was after midnight, a beautiful starlit summer night. The belfry of the chapel stood out in the ghostly night light of the western sky. The white of women's legs could be seen straddled on graves. In the distance dogs barked and from the direction of Drumnay the hoarse voices of men going home echoed across the still night valleys.

Alone in the shadow of the hedge the thought of the farm came back to Tarry. His mother was the wisest of them all. He saw this night what would happen to a man who went down the banks. As his mother often said – 'what the blackbird whistled to Paddy McNamee was true – have it or do without it.'

Eusebius wouldn't lend him a bare fourpence and he had it on him.

Tarry was planning the next day's work. He would not let his stuff go to loss in future. He promised himself to stop smoking. He threw away the butt he had in his mouth as a tribute to his promise.

One of the couples returned from the graveyard, the man with his raincoat wrapped over the heads of himself and the girl. Charlie had a raincoat just like that, but you couldn't be sure.

A briar bent down and touched him on the nose. The briars were friendly. He took it as a warning to move off a distance. If he were seen lingering there for long someone might say he was up to nothing good. If one of the bicycles were stolen he might be blamed.

A number of men who had been up in the public house returned to the hall half drunk. Among them was the priest's brother and Mary. If Tarry hadn't been fully engaged thinking of his farm and the hay which he had to rope the next day, he would have been more worried.

His mother would find a big change in him tomorrow. No more nonsense. The land. He began to hum a poem that was in one of his school books.

> Oh the summer night has a smile of light
> As she sits on her sapphire throne.

The words applied to this night. The hills silhouetted against the horizon of pale stars belonged to a world where men like the men whom Tarry knew did not exist. The scent of the woodbine and the richer smell of the potato-stalks came across the valley and he knew something that made a man happy in the midst of desolation. Another group now began to congregate around the door of the dance hall to see the swanks emerge.

Larry Finnegan was there and Tarry could not help thinking that he, an old married man, was hardly waiting merely to see the dancers come out. Two of his own daughters were at the dance but it was unlikely that he would be watching them. No, there was only one thing could have kept him out of his bed and that was the chance of getting a kick at Tarry.

It turned out that the Finnegans did not want to injure their case by an attack on Tarry and the result was that they fell between two stools.

The dancers poured out from the hall.

Tarry watched the girls happy in the knowledge that the only one he really cared for had no boy friend with her. It seemed almost too good to be true. Eusebius did not appear though Tarry waited till the last person had come out. He was about to go home when staring sharply into a gap in the hedge where bicycles were stacked he saw Eusebius drag his bicycle out and after that a girl's machine. Without pretending that he saw his friend, Eusebius took the two bicycles and went off in the opposite direction. The girl's bicycle was Mary Reilly's; he could tell the whirr of its free-wheel.

Tarry was too tired to feel the worst pains of jealousy; and he was inclined to be glad that it was Eusebius who was leaving the girl home. Eusebius was a decent fellow whatever else he was – and he was sure to bore the girl.

I'll bet, mused Tarry as he went home, that Eusebius will talk poetry to her. He was experienced enough to know that only those who did not feel the spirit deeply could make it pay romantic dividends.

With loving hands he was drawing the light American rake

round the last of the hay cocks, his mind relishing the thought that a finer built cock of hay than the one he had just headed and roped he had not seen for a long time. All the seventeen cocks were well built – and the right well-saved hay it was; those cocks wouldn't take a bit of hurt if they were left out for a month. He stood out from the cock and ran his eye up and down the sides of it. A grand job. There would be about seven hundred-weight of hay in every cock. He dropped the rake and pulled out a wisp of the hay and sniffed it.

May alive, that *was* hay. The cow that would be fed on that wouldn't take a founder – she would not.

The shame and degradation of the night before was being buried in a pile of fresh sweet-smelling hay. What might he care about a bunch of ignorant fools that would hardly know when they'd have their fill eaten. He was in the best of form; he never felt as fit in his life.

What about putting up a high jump?

He stood the fork in the hard ground and put the rake standing while he made a thumb-rope of the hay. He took pride in his skill at making a thumb-rope. As he drew the hay out of the cock and twisted it with his thumb and with a second movement wound the rope into a ball, he knew that as well as knowing the magic that was in the world he could show the best of the farmers a thing or two. *There* was a thumb-rope and a half, as thin as a plough-rein – Aw, man!

He made the rope the cross-bar of the high jump at a height which reached the third button of his waistcoat – or where the third button would be if he were wearing his waistcoat. It couldn't be less than four feet ten or eleven. If he could get over that jump he'd be in good form.

He slipped off his boots and danced about gingerly on the silvery stubbles. The ground was a bit too hard for jumping, but two or three tries couldn't kill him. On his first attempt he failed. He knew he could do it. There was nobody about. Nobody could see him here – except by a miracle, the Bradys – so he took off his trousers and knotted his shirt between his legs. He built his will up till his imagination towered over the jump. He knew he could do it now. Lovely, lovely, he said to himself as he crossed the jump cleanly and came down on one leg facing it. He let himself sprawl away to get the full pleasure out of his feat. He raised the rope. This time he would try a jump the height of his chin. If he could get over that one he might well say he was in form. How about taking off the shirt? It wasn't very heavy but it hobbled him somewhat about the legs. He was stripped to the skin. Before making the attempt he searched the thin places in the hedge and scanned the point of McKenna's hill to make sure that no one was looking.

Oh, good God! Molly was standing on top of the dunghill and she surely could see through a hole in the hedge. She was watching, there was no doubt about it. Well, let her look away, thought he: she can't see very much from that range. Yet, it might be as well if he put on his trousers. It was always a risk going about in one's pelt. He remembered how he was caught one morning before when he got up at about four of a summer's morning to see about the mare due to foal and he didn't bother putting a stitch on him – and May Callan saw him as he ran across the meadow. She was coming from a dance.

Better be on the safe side. He put on his trousers and his boots and decided to abandon athletics for the day. He let the jump remain so that he could contemplate his prowess. He was very proud of his jump.

He sat down beside the cock, took a drink out of the little can of thick milk and lit a cigarette. He crawled away from the cock to where his jacket lay and got out the book on phrenology, which was folded in the inside pocket. He read about Wendell Phillips, 'the silver-tongued orator', and as he read, dreaming that he was that 'silver-tongued orator', he felt his skull but doubted if it was the right shape and size.

'Hello.'

He swung round on his backside.

It was Molly.

'How did you get here?' he asked, displeased.

'I climbed through the bushes at the top.'

He did not want to see the trollop. His mind was hard and

clear and the athlete in him had no interest in short-legged women.

'Don't sit down there or you'll put the cock to the hollow. If you want to sit at all sit on the hill-side of it.'

The hill-side of the cock was a bunch of briars and Molly had to stand.

'My mother,' said Molly, 'asked me to ask you if you could lend us the rake to gather the bog bedding that we got cut last week.'

'I couldn't give you the good *American* rake, Molly, but there's a thick-set wire-toothed one at home – if it would be any use to yous.'

Molly said that that rake would do fine. The rake was only an excuse.

'I'm going away,' said she suddenly.

'What the hell are you doing that for?'

'Amn't I as well? Look at the way your two sisters went. There's nothing for a lassie in these parts.' She hesitated a moment and then said: 'Do you remember that evening we were together up the oul' road, Tarry?'

'What night?' said he sourly.

'You know well, Tarry.'

'I don't know what you're talking about, I just don't know what you're talking about. I do know that you were out one or two nights with Charlie, but you were never out with *me*.'

He was disturbed. This sort of thing took all the good out of life. He didn't like the attitude the girl adopted. There was a toughness about her, like the toughness of one who in her own defence would swear a man's life away, and he was afraid. He was afraid to think what he was thinking and he shoved the thought back into his mind.

The girl straggled off and he let her go without another word of farewell or of anything.

This was only one of the worries that were congregating around his happiness, trying to drive it away. There were the Finnegans, both families, who were only waiting to attack him; there was the question of the new farm with the transfer deed still not completed, and now this.

He put his hand in his trouser pocket and looked at his one and sixpence. He had often said it before and he said it now again – the whole problem was scarcity of money. If he had some money he could go away for a week and when he'd have come back all the cares would have dispersed.

He chewed at a weed. He watched a beetle creeping through the rutted earth. He lifted a flat stone and underneath was a nest of pismires. A pity he hadn't got Molly to sit on them.

Clouds blew across the blue sky. He wouldn't mind if it rained now that he had his hay safe and Eusebius had not.

'Tarry, are you alive or dead?'

He sprang to his feet and grabbed the fork and rake on hearing his mother's voice. She had brought him his tea.

She was in good humour, very pleased and proud as she surveyed the field full of cocks. 'I can only count sixteen,' she said and she had her palm edged over her brow.

He put the navvy can of tea beside him and swallowed the bread in a hurry. 'There's seventeen if you count again,' he said.

'Aw yes, the one in the corner.'

'The best hay in your country,' he said.

'Let others do the praising, Tarry. Nothing I hate as much as a man that's always boasting about his own things. There's that Mrs Callan and nobody has anything but her to hear her talking. Her three skinny cows give more milk and butter than anyone else's. I say – Did this May get much of a show at the dance last night?'

'She was only danced three times,' said Tarry to please his mother.

'And what about our Bridie?'

'*She* got a great show.'

'That atself. Was this slob on the hill at it?'

'I didn't see her.'

'Poor slob. Keep away from her anyway. Last Sunday her mother had hardly an eye to see me coming from Mass and ... What had you the thumb-rope for?'

'Doing a bit of measuring, aye.'

'Aye, too. Were you speaking to Father Markey last night?'

162

'Of course I was. Don't you know very well I was?'

'I'm glad to hear it. I like keeping in with the priests. You never know when you'd want one of them to do you a good turn. And God forgive me some of them could do you a bad turn as quick as a good one. Don't stay too long, I may want you to give me a hand with the churning. I hope these ones of ours make a fist of the eating-house. You'll not be long.'

'Be home in an hour.'

When she had gone a short distance she turned and called back, 'Do you know, I was told that one of the Dillon's was having another youngster. Did you hear anything about it?'

He didn't.

'There may be nothing about it. Ah, God protect everybody's rearing. I got Bridie to drive up the two-year-old bullocks to Carlin's this morning, what was the use letting the grass go to loss?'

'I'll be home shortly,' Tarry said to get her away.

'Mind you don't leave the fork or rake behind you for someone to whip.'

'They'll be safe.'

He went home feeling more at ease with the world than he had felt for a long time. In spite of all his worries the warm and gay heart of life was beating for him. New flowers were coming up and new scents and smells.

Around the house, for a wonder, there was peace. He threw the old book in a corner of the horses' stable and went into the house.

His mother was sitting by the hearth with her head between her palms on her knees. His sister, Mary, had come out from the town and was sitting with a pout near the bottom of the stairs.

'What the devil's wrong?' he asked on entering.

'This is more of your reading of the books,' said the mother without raising her head. 'Two of the darling bullocks that nothing would do you but to leave up in Carlin's are bad with the blackleg.'

'The blackleg, good God! It can't be cured,' he said.

'Just when things were going to pick up,' lamented the mother.

'That's a terror. I better get the rest of them vaccinated.'

'I sent for a man to do it,' said the mother. 'I suppose, like everything else, you'd take on to do that too.'

'That's a terror,' Tarry kept repeating.

'There's always some trouble here,' said the mother. 'If it's not one thing it's the other. I only came back from the hay-field when Bridie had this news for me. And to add to me trouble this one here is back from the town saying that they can't get any trade – with all their cookery books.'

The mother had sent Bridie up to Cassidy's to ask Eusebius to put the vaccination pellets in the remaining cattle, Eusebius having a punch for that purpose. She had also made plans to get Charlie to take the dead beasts which would be cheaper than burying them; and it would do Charlie a good turn, for by all accounts in the new butcher's shop which he had opened he needed no slaughterhouse.

'I'm chucking the whole damn thing,' he said to Eusebius when they were vaccinating the cattle.

'Keep a good grip on them horns, Tarry,' said Eusebius. 'Chucking what?'

'Drumnay.'

'You are in me arse?'

'I am,' said Tarry, without really meaning what he was saying – at least he did not think he meant it. 'And then you can have all the women to yourself, and all the land as well. I don't give a tuppeny damn for the whole thing.'

Eusebius registered pleasure, Tarry could see that. He would be pleased to see a man leave the district, one rival less.

That day passed and another day and something was wrong in Tarry's life, something was driving him – where, he did not know. Something was pulling him back, but he did know what that was, and he was seeing it now when he lifted his eyes to the lonely hills.

8

If any born of kindlier blood
Should ask what maiden lies below –
Say only this: A tender bud
That tried to blossom in the snow
Lies withered where the violets blow.

The bottom of the page which contained this poem was encrusted with dried cow-dung and the pages were stuck together in the same way. Tarry shoved the old book between the rafters and galvanized roof of the horse stable, and completed the buttoning of his trousers. The sunlight was beaming through the stable door but it was at the light seen through the slit in the wall over the manger that Tarry was looking. A large nettle waved to and fro in front of the slit almost humanly. He lit a cigarette and took several deep pulls, for he was starved for a smoke.

His mother was standing at the road gate gossiping with Mrs Callan. These two women delighted in giving each other the quiet dig and in these arguments Tarry's mother seldom got the worst of it. But on this morning Tarry didn't particularly like the way his mother appeared to be reacting.

'Bridgie,' she said as they parted, 'it would fit us all a lot better if we minded our own business.'

The mother went into the house and Tarry heard her inquiring where 'this blackguard' was. She must have thought either himself or Bridie was upstairs. He sucked hard at the cigarette, dropped it into a wet piece of hen manure and went into the house taking with him a pair of hames, which he was examining with a very concerned air. 'I have to fix the hook on these hames,' he muttered and put on a worried farmer's face.

Mrs Flynn was stooped on the centre of the floor over a fat hen which she held between her knees, and which she was about to kill for the next day's dinner. Under the hen was an enamel basin.

'Give me that knife off the ground,' she snapped at her son. She cut the head off the hen and hung the bird on the back of the dairy door with the basin under it. She wiped the carving knife in her apron and then opened up:

'Hell won't be full till you're in it. Hell won't be full till you're in it. To think that a man that never saw nothing but what was right in this house should have us the talk of the country. Oh, his uncle Petey all over again.'

Tarry was on all fours under the table. 'I can't get that hammer,' he said at last as he withdrew his head and stood up. He pretended not to have heard. 'Night, noon and morning, it's me that's sick, sore and sorry with the whole lot of yous,' said the mother.

'What's wrong?' said Tarry, very surprised.

'What in the Name of Father, Son and Holy Ghost had you to do with this Molly one?' said she, suiting her voice to the seriousness of the charge. She was speaking slowly and rather softly and all the more terrifying for that.

'I don't know what you're coming at,' he said with the pout of a man in a hurry to do some important business who was displeased at being interrupted by trifling affairs. 'If I knew where that bleddy hammer is I wouldn't care.' His eyes swept into dusty corners and he moved the six-gallon pot from its place in the corner of the hob and looked behind it.

The mother sat by the fire on the low stool and blew her nose defiantly into the ashes.

Speaking in a low solemn voice she began to say:

'Never had a day's comfort in me whole life. Never a day that I hadn't some misfortune to contend with. Oh, it's me that reared the family I should be proud of. Will you leave that pair of hames there, and if they want repairs bring them to the forge and not knock an eye out of your head like poor Joe McArdle. You be to have some curse o' God carry-on with her or this sneak up the road wouldn't have it. And sure it's only now its dawning on me why oul' Molly hasn't an eye to see me last Sunday coming from Mass, one that always had a little story for me.'

'I never went near her in me whole life,' said Tarry with

166

the weakness of an innocent man. 'Never, never, never. I wouldn't go near her if I was paid for it – you ought to know *that?*'

He wandered to the door in the hope of escaping the torture, and as he stepped outside the postman was getting off his bicycle. The mother, too deeply in argument, had missed him coming up the road, which was a wonder. Tarry slipped quietly to the gate and collected a letter which was addressed to himself. He stood in the doorway of the carthouse and hurriedly scanned the letter. It was from the solicitor who was dealing with the transfer of Carlin's farm to the Flynns, and it said that there appeared to be some trouble over the boundaries of the holding. Two fields appeared not to be included in the purchased property. Would Tarry and his mother call to his office some day soon? Tarry stuffed the letter in his pocket and returned to the house with a very innocent look.

'You got a letter,' said she at once.

'Who said I got a letter?'

'Isn't there the postman going back the road?'

'Must be in Cassidy's he was.'

'I thought it might be this rodney of an uncle of yours who was threatening to come back to lie up on us – we're not bad enough.'

Tarry was too deeply shocked over the news contained in the letter to be able to conceal his distress from his mother. She, however, thought that his nervousness was due to the scandal about Molly, which was only what she would expect.

'Hang on that six-gallon pot till I make a drop of gruel for the calves and bring up a couple of goes of water from the bog-hole to wash the praties for the dinner. Oh, never during soot was there such a family as mine, one worse, than the other ... The dirty pot-walloper,' she was referring to Molly now, 'sure it's not that I'd care a hair if you had to keep away from her. And you needn't try to tell me that you did, for I saw you with me own two eyes no later than a month ago when you were running the turnips. How many a night last winter when she used to call here on her ceilidhe did you not sneak out and it used to make me

167

laugh the way you thought we didn't know. Yes, standing down there at the corner of the back garden with the rain pouring down, I could hear you sighing. Sure, you needn't think we're all blind. Yes, waiting for her to lave till you'd waylay her.'

Tarry could not deny this allegation, which was quite true.

If his mother only knew he was now rather pleased that she had this lesser of the two evils to engage her attention until such time as things straightened out. He was wondering if Eusebius wasn't behind this business of the land. He must have known something or he'd have been more jealous at the time of purchase. Tarry would inform his mother right away if he thought that she could find a way out of the dilemma.

He poured a bucket of water into the pot and the mother twisted the bellows' wheel. 'If you'd tell me,' said she, 'you might find that I'd be a better advice than some of these cute customers up the road with their ballads and the devil knows what. How well Eusebius never gets his name up with anything. He's in with everybody. Don't slash the water all over the floor. Oh, Eusebius knows how to mind number one.

'And another thing,' said the mother while poking the fire under the pot, 'it's about time we heard from that solicitor about the farm. One of these days I must go out meself and see him and find what's keeping him with that deed. I never liked the look of that man even if he is Father Daly's cousin. I hope you put the haggard in order for the hay atself.'

'I did, I did.'

Bridie arrived at this point. She came in through the dairy and as she was closing the door behind her the mother called to her to bring up a plateful of barley meal to put on the pot. But Bridie had something on her mind and first rushed to the kitchen saying: 'Did you hear about pet Tarry?'

'What talk with you?' said the mother.

'His name all over the country with Molly,' said Bridie.

'He never had a haporth to do with the targer, Bridie, you whipster, you, and how dar' you say he had?'

Bridie shook her shoulders with a jeer and went for the meal. Her mother's voice pursued her: 'Choke you and double choke you, he never left a hand on the trollop. Have we not enough trouble without you putting in your cutty?'

Tarry went outside to think. He deceived himself into believing that he could think himself out of his various problems. He walked to the road gate consciously thinking – but nothing was happening in his mind. The threatened lawcase by the Finnegans had petered out, but no thanks to his thinking. There was a worldly wisdom which looked so much like stupidity that he could not tolerate it. He had seen and observed the worldly-wise men of the place with their platitudes and their unoriginality, and he knew that he could never bring himself to act as they acted. Eusebius was coming down the road whistling 'Does Your Mother Come from Ireland'. Eusebius was a man who combined the stupidity of the world with a veneer of the other-world gaiety, and as Tarry waited for him to come up he was wondering how it was that a man could see all this worldliness and observe its workings, and yet be quite incapable of using it himself.

It was the same in matters concerning women. Nobody knew more than Tarry about the theories of love, and nobody was more foolish when it came to practising them.

'Sound man, Eusebius,' said Tarry leaning over the gate.

Eusebius took the hay fork off his shoulder and used it to lean on. He glanced at the sky: 'Do you think will it howl out?'

'I think so,' said Tarry.

Tarry could see that his neighbour was bursting with delight at his misfortune, but he needed someone in whom to confide, and Eusebius had that soft, easy, feminine way with him which was so deceptive, so dangerous, and which could suck information out of the least confiding of men. Considering the matter, Tarry realized that Eusebius knew more about him than any other man or woman alive. How much did he know of Eusebius' private life? Practically nothing. On the other hand was there such a lot to know? Tarry consoled himself with the thought that there was not. And the surprising thing, thought Tarry between the words they were speaking, was that Eusebius never came without some sensational gossip. He was always confessing his sins, but the sum did not add up to anything a man could remember.

'Anything strange on your travels, Eusebius?'

'Curse o' God on the haporth, Tarry, if you haven't something yourself. Why, did you hear something?'

Tarry opened the gate and went to the middle of the road where he stood and stretched his arms and yawned as if filled with the greatest indifference to Drumnay and Dargan and life in general. 'I had a mind to draw in the hay the morrow,' he yawned.

'Nothing like it, Tarry. Begod,' said Eusebius looking narrowly at Tarry, 'I have a kind of notion you heard something funny. Don't be so bleddy close. Go and tell a fella.' He prodded the gravel with the prongs of the fork. 'You heard something?'

'Don't you know very well I'd tell you if I heard anything, Eusebius, don't you know that?'

'You might,' nodded Eusebius doubtfully, and started to make a pattern on the road with the fork prongs.

'Well, and it's hardly worth me while telling you, I was only thinking you might have heard something about the Brady one. She wasn't seen at Mass this past month, and people are talking, do you see?'

'I see,' said Eusebius as if he were hearing something very sensational.

Tarry gave a sickly laugh designed to throw cold water on the story as a story. 'And the funny thing is,' said he with the same unhealthy laugh, 'some people were trying to say that I was seen with her. Wouldn't that make you laugh, heh? Of course it's all Charlie's doing – wouldn't you say?'

'Jabus, that's a dread,' said Eusebius, 'that bates the little dish as the fellow said. And are you doing anything about it?'

'Sure the thing isn't worth talking about,' said Tarry fluttering his hands to show the limit of carelessness. 'Sure, Holy God ...'

He stopped talking to let Paddy Callan who was mooching suspiciously on the other side of the hedge, pretending he was examining his oats, but trying to hear what was being said – a habit of his – pass.

170

'It's coming in nicely,' sang out Eusebius with his affected gaiety to Paddy. 'It should be in for the Fifteenth, Paddy?'

'What's that you said, young fella?' inquired Paddy.

'You have a good crop of oats, Paddy, except that wee spot on the scrugan that's a bit short of itself.'

'It'll have to be doing,' said Paddy philosophically.

Tarry as usual was impatient to get rid of the intruder and showed it by signs that would be obvious to the blindest ass.

Paddy took the hint, but before going winked at Eusebius as much as to say – 'who'd think he had it in him?'

'Yes – ?' said Eusebius to Tarry.

'There's no doubt about it I can't help laughing when I think of it. Wouldn't it make you laugh, Eusebius? now wouldn't it?'

Eusebius was very doubtful and disinclined to comfort his neighbour. 'They say the woman's word is law,' he said.

'Not always, Eusebius. You remember the case that was reported in the *Anglo-Celt*, and it was the man's word that was taken. Come down the road a bit, I don't want that mother of mine to be coming out. I'll fight it to the last ditch. I'll fight it.'

'What else would you do? You'd need to get a first-class man.'

'Oh, I know some of the young fellas, Eusebius, they wouldn't be so dear.'

Eusebius was emphatic that an experienced counsel would be necessary. 'I could tell you your best plan only I don't know enough about the case, Tarry. There's no use in making up lies, you know.'

'She can go to hell backwards,' declared Tarry,' they can get nothing off me. You can't take feathers off a frog, heh?'

'You have Carlin's.'

'Maybe I have.'

Eusebius put the fork on his shoulder and hurried off. 'I might see you coming back,' Tarry called after him.

He could tell by the bones in the back of Eusebius' neck which moved like the hips of a gamy woman that his neighbour was a happy man – happy in a next-door neighbour's misfortune.

171

Eusebius danced along the road kicking the pebbles before him. Tarry had to admit to himself that had their positions been reversed he would have been happy too. Hating one's next-door neighbour was an essential part of a small farmer's religion. Hate and jealousy made love – even the love of land – an exciting adventure.

If any man of them in that country were to open his eyes, if the fog in which they lived lifted, they would be unable to endure the futility of it all. Their courage was the courage of the blind. But Tarry had seen beyond the fog the Eternal light shining on the stones.

As he was clearing away the stones and rubbish from the haggard he thought the scene so enchanting that he sometimes felt that there must be something the matter with him. The three big nettles that grew in the ring of boulders upon which last year's pikes of hay had stood were rich with the beauty of what is richly alive. The dust of last year's hay and straw was so lovely it could almost make him want to prostrate himself upon it. Stones, clay, grass, the sunlight coming through the privet hedge. Why did he love such common things? He was ashamed of mentioning his love; these things were not supposed to be beautiful.

He scraped the dusty straw with the shovel and looked with admiration at the clean brown floor of the haggard.

He left the shovel standing against the hedge and stared across the townland towards his own fields. He could see the blue glint of the spraying stuff on the leaves of the potatoes and far in the distance of his farm the movements of the mare and her foal on the far side of a thick hedge.

Old Molly Brady's shadow passed along the horizon at the back of her house; she looked contented enough. He turned his eyes to the hills on his left and saw with delight Callan's scabby field of turnips. He tried to find in the badness of this neighbour's crop a counter-irritant for his own troubles but it was no use.

He wandered into the cabbage garden to cool his mind in the ever-wet green cool leaves.

172

> Under the broad leaves of cabbages how cool
> Even in the middle of July the clay is –
> Like ice-cream.

He nibbled at the caraway seeds that grew in the hedgerow running his mind back to the days of his peacefulness. It was like this that all terrible things happened to a man – casually. Thus a man might find himself with a broken neck or on trial for murder and he'd wonder how he arrived at such a place.

So far the affair with Molly was only a rumour. Tarry himself only knew about it from the gossip of the neighbours. He had seen the girl and her mother since the rumour had gone abroad, and on one occasion had nearly got up enough courage to put it to the test. But he was afraid of putting things to the test; it was better to live in doubt – which is the same as hope – than to have all one's doubts and fears proven well-founded.

The last time he had been speaking to the girl Molly was about three weeks before when she was in her usual good spirits, and her mother bantered him from the height behind the house as he spoke to Molly at the well.

It might be put down as a remarkable fact that during all this time it never occurred to Tarry, or his mother for that matter, that the Bradys might be expecting someone – even Tarry – to marry the girl; that is, if there was anything the matter with her at all. At this moment the thought that the girl did want to get married flashed through Tarry's thoughts, but his egotistical mind could no more entertain it seriously than it could anything in the shape of genuine sympathy for anyone but himself. He had moments in which he saw himself as he was, but he knew that he had his justification. There were some people who were fit for nothing else but to sympathize, but a man like himself had a dispensation from such side-tracking activities.

A man who had seen the ecstatic light of Life in stones, on the hills, in leaves of cabbages and weeds was not bound by the pity of Christ.

Or was he?

If he were, how much that was great in literature and art would be lost. He justified himself by the highest examples he knew of.

Is self-pity not pity for mankind as seen in one man? He had it all off. But, O God! if he could only transport himself down the years, three years into the future when all would be forgotten. The present tied him in its cruel knots and dragged him through bushes and briars, stones and weeds on his mouth and nose.

They got half the hay home the next day, and would have done better seeing that Paddy Reilly had sent a man with a hay slide, but the rain came on in the early evening when the pike was at its widest. Tarry, who had heard that the wireless had said the evening before that there would be no rain, was yet not caught entirely unprepared. He had three nice lumps of cocks of bottom hay in the meadow right beside the haggard, and with this bottom hay they were able to put a good heart in the pike. Over the mound they spread a winnowing sheet, and when they went in for their tea Tarry was trying to think of all the men whose hay pikes had been caught at their widest in the downpour and with no winnowing sheets or bottom hay near at hand.

'I think,' said he to his mother later, 'I'll go up as far as Carlin's and see about them heifers that's in calf.' In-calf heifers and cows were not subject to the blackleg, and it was this class of animal that the Flynns had put to graze on the new farm since the bullocks took the disease and died.

The mother felt that Tarry was now taking her advice and attending to his place, but when she saw him go to the top of the dresser when he thought she wasn't looking and slip an old book into his pocket she wasn't so sure. She said nothing, for Paddy Reilly's man had jumped up just then saying: 'It's time for me to be looking for feet.'

Tarry threw a corn sack over his shoulders and took his bicycle out of the car-house. The mother came out and said: 'If they're lying don't put them up, for I don't think there's any danger of them having the red water, and some of them are heavy in calf.'

Tarry laid his bicycle against the stone fence of the first of his fields alongside the lane that led to Carlin's and Joe Finnegan's, and was about to spring over the fence when Jemmy Carlin, the silent sneerer of the family, came rushing from his street with a rusty graip in his hands which he had poised like a javelin and bawled: 'Trespassers will be prosecuted, trespassers will be prosecuted.'

Tarry stood taking in the situation. He had plenty of experience with Joe Finnegan, but somehow this looked more dangerous, more like business, than anything Joe had done.

He got down off the stone fence and stood with the bicycle between him and his approaching enemy.

'I'll put the grains of this graip in your guts, you grabber, if you put a foot inside me fields.'

'What fields?' said Tarry, wondering.

'My fields, avic.'

'Didn't we buy them, Jemmy?'

'Buy *my* fields,' sneered Jemmy, 'sure yous couldn't buy my good fields. You bought Tom's farm, but you didn't buy mine. By God, you didn't buy mine, and you couldn't buy mine.' The man settled some mossy stones on the fence with an air of ownership. 'Buy my good fields, buy my good fields,' he kept saying.

'Let me drive the cattle to the drink atself.'

'I drove them to the field with the drink in it, avic, and I may as well tell you that if they put their noses into one or other of these two good fields of mine they'll calve before their time.'

'But how am I going to get to them?' Tarry appealed.

'Go round the lane the way that any dacent man id go.'

With that Jemmy moved off along the fence, shifting a stone here and picking up a dead branch there while Tarry stood by his bicycle beginning to understand the mistake they had made in purchasing the farm without having the boundaries properly defined. He suddenly remembered too that day in Shercock when he had bought a second-hand copy of the poems of Byron and how Eusebius had said it was 'bleddy fine', but himself bought an Ordnance Map of Drumnay and Miskin.

Tarry was forced to walk with his bicycle round the narrow, rutted, muddy lane that led past the back of Finnegan's house, and down along the field of potatoes. It had been one of his causes for thankfulness that he didn't need to use this old lane about which the Finnegans were forever grumbling. The gate that had to be closed every time you went through would be enough to keep the lawyers in trade for the rest of their lives. The lane at the back of Finnegan's led through the bottom of a dunghill, and the briars that hung overhead were often decorated with the bits of dung which caught there when Joe was flinging dung out of the cow house.

Tarry got safely past the bottom of Carlin's garden and he hardly cared what happened to him as he picked his steps and sometimes had to carry his bicycle over some parts of the lane. He knew that he would have a poor chance of getting past Finnegan's with the five small girls and the mother who was so starved for gossip that she would be liable to spot anything in the shape of news. The row he had had with Joe Finnegan was liable to flare up again. Joe was sure to have heard about the mistake in the boundary and would be delighted with the chance of pouncing on a man who was down.

Tarry was surprised and grateful when Joe who was barrowing rotten mangolds from his haggard and dumping them on the side of the pane behind the house merely gave a loud forced laugh as he passed. 'Oh, ho, the big farmer,' he cried wildly. 'Hah, hah, hah, hah,' he laughed.

Tarry hurried on expecting every moment to have a stone or at least a rotten mangold hopped off his head, but the man let him pass on, apparently contented to be a spectator of a most enjoyable play.

Tarry didn't need to make a close examination of the property to know how much of it was his. The two best fields which comprised more than the half and which alone gave access to the lane at the point west of Carlin's had been fenced off ostentatiously by Jemmy Carlin that day with large green whitethorn bushes, and the cattle had been driven without concern for their condition into the other section of the property. They were lying in the wet soaking mud, bedraggled looking as if they had been roughly driven – which no doubt they were – out of the two good fields. There were bits of briar and bushes stuck in their tails

176

showing that they had been forced through the heavily bushed gaps out of which the bushes had not been first removed.

Three of the five fields which remained were bounded for a considerable length by Finnegan's, the last thing Tarry or his mother would want. The five fields were composed of soil as poor as was to be found in the county Cavan – which was saying a good deal, and without the two good ones to balance them out they would be a millstone around any purchaser's neck. The cattle hated the sour grass which grew in them, and the only saving feature was the drink in them. Indeed, so wet was the soil that even in the middle of summer they could get a drink from the pools that formed on the spongy heights.

What would Tarry tell his mother? It was on his advice she had paid over the bulk of the purchase money – two hundred pounds – and it was doubtful if they could get any of that money back now. Didn't they buy it with their eyes open would be said.

'Well, how are they?' she inquired when he returned.

'All fine,' he answered.

'That atself. There's a bit of rice there in the pot that I made for you, you must be tired after pitching that hay. The best of a farm if it was minded. Two of as good a fields ...' Tarry was stooped over the pot of rice, trying to forget.

The mother stayed in the kitchen making bread. Tarry went upstairs and sat beside the old Howe sewing machine – the father of all sewing machines – in the corner of the room facing the front window.

This corner was his Parnassus, the constant point above time. Winter and summer since his early boyhood he had sat here and the lumps of candle-grease on the scaly table of the old machine told a story.

He carried out his usual ritual, for the Muse is attracted and held by the little gestures just as women are. Beside him he arranged the verses which he knew would excite him – at the right moment. He had *Madame Bovary* within reach. His method of getting a thrill out of this book and of all exciting books was

177

not by reading them through, but by opening them at random and giving a quick look inside. Then he would shut the book again lest the magic should escape. He crossed his legs, got out the puce pencil and the blue notepaper and let his mind become passive.

A thrush was singing his plagiarized version of the blackbird's song in one of the poplars behind the house. Callan's hill, all white with Michaelmas daisies, looked in at him. For a moment his passive mind was being wooed by the clump of black sallies at the bottom of the garden. In among the sallies on the shaky scraw there were water-hens hopping.

The net of earthly intrigue could not catch him here. He was on a level with the horizon – and it was a level on which there was laughter. Looking down at his own misfortunes he thought them funny now. From this height he could even see himself losing his temper with the Finnegans and the Carlins and hating his neighbours and he moved the figures on the landscape, made them speak, and was filled with joy in his own power.

> The rattle of buckets, rolling of barrels under
> Down-spouts, the leading in of foals
> Were happenings caught in wonder
> The stones white with rain were living souls.

He was in his secret room in the heart now. Having entered he could be bold. A man hasn't to be on his best behaviour in Heaven; he can kick the furniture around. He can stoop down and pick up lumps of mortality without being born again to die.

Tarry rose from his chair and began to search under his bed. He dragged out a large black wooden box, one of the old boxes in which his mother's trousseau had come. This box was filled with papers and faded documents – old letters, rent receipts, bills, the *Anglo-Celt* for the year 1905.

He pulled out a bundle of the papers and spread them on the bed and then got sitting beside them very caressingly.

Here were two long damp-stained envelopes. Within was the correspondence over the right o' way to Finnegan's well which

178

had been such a bone of contention between the families forty years before. The Flynns won that law suit – and as was often the case with the winners they were more bitter than the losers, and Tarry's grandfather had encouraged him to carry on the feud. Tarry had been taught how mean and low the Finnegans were when in fact they were only amusing. One of the letters from the solicitor for the Finnegans said: 'My client denies the alleged assault on your wife. When your wife came to the well my client remonstrated with her for leaving the gate to the well open so that the cattle in the fields could go down and pollute the spring. My client absolutely denies that she pulled your wife's hair out; the hairs, if any, which were found on the bushes were not hairs from your wife's head but from the tails of the cattle which your wife's carelessness caused to get down to the well.'

When he was replacing the letters in their envelopes he noticed another small note inside. Taking it out he found that it was a letter from his uncle Petey dated nineteen nineteen and addressed from West Africa to Tarry's mother. It was a pleasant childish hand much faded now, but Tarry could make out that the man was asking for money in the most oblique way possible. He had nine hundred and ninety pounds he said and all he wanted was the other ten to buy some great bargain – something to do with a mine. How his mother must have sneered at that letter.

'Holy smoke,' said Tarry dreamingly aloud. He put the correspondence back in the box and shoved it under the bed with his foot. Then he sat down at the machine again and lit a candle.

He wrote about his own room:

> Ten by twelve
> And a low roof,
> If I stand by the side-wall
> My head feels the reproof.
> Five holy pictures
> Hang on the walls:
> The Virgin and Child,
> St Anthony of Padua,
> Leo the XIII,
> St Patrick and the Little Flower.

His mother had been out of the house a few minutes talking to somebody at the gate. Presently she walked slowly towards the dunghill, and as she passed the window Tarry knew that she had heard something. She came in in the company of Bridie who had the milk with her, and having put the vessel on the bottom step of the stairs cried in a broken voice:

'Tarry, Tarry, Tarry. Are you in or are you out?'

He rattled on the floor with his feet.

'Oh, what in the wide earthly world are we to do at all?' she cried, and there was no fake about her emotion now. If all belonging to her had died suddenly she could not have been more disturbed. Tarry jumped up from his seat and went down to console her.

'What is the matter, mother?'

'God! O God! O God!' she lamented, 'and you told me that you saw the map and knew everything!'

'What's the matter?'

'Everything's the matter, everything's the matter. Oh, I was better dead and in the boneyard than have to put up with this. Oh, it's me that's to be pitied if ever a woman was to be pitied!'

'Try to pull yourself together,' said Tarry. 'Is it over Carlin's?'

'Is it over Carlin's? Lord! O Lord! Oh I was better dead and buried, a thousand times better.'

Bridie, straining the milk in the dairy, beckoned to her brother to come outside and let the temper wear off the mother. 'It's the only cure for it,' she said.

They sat together on a bag of bran in the dairy, and Bridie confessed to her brother for the first time that the parish of Dargan, and the people in it, was no place for a civilized man or woman. 'A girl was better sell herself openly on the streets of a city,' she declared.

'What do you think of the Molly one?' Tarry asked.

'What the hell about it?' said Bridie quietly. 'What the hell do you care if you had nothing to do with her, and even if you had for that matter.' They listened. 'She's slowing down a bit now. Don't say one word when you go up now.'

'Not a word,' Tarry promised.

The mother's crying and sighing died down and the brother and sister went up to the kitchen, moving about the floor on tip-toes and saying nothing.

Tarry was being very good but he could not restrain himself from taking a nip out of the cake of raisin bread that stood on the dresser. His sister grinned her disapproval, but Tarry ate away, and afterwards took a drink out of the cream jug where the fresh milk had been put for the breakfast.

Bridie was disgusted. 'You'll start her off again,' she whispered viciously.

'Leave us alone,' he said.

The clock ticked on in the room. The cat climbed up on the dresser and began to fumble among the plates.

'Put that cat down,' said the mother, raising her head from her knees.

They were half way through the Rosary when the mother knelt straight up and listened. Tarry awoke and listened too. A motor car was coming slowly up the Drumnay road, its slow purr ominous, like news of death.

Tarry changed colours. The mother sat up and stuck her feet in her shoes. They waited anxiously to see if the car would go past the gate. Next thing they heard the rattle of the gate and a man's voice guiding the driver who was driving through to turn the car in the street.

'Father, Son and Holy Ghost!' prayed the mother, 'did something happen to one of these in Shercock? One trouble never comes alone.'

Tarry dashed to the door. Bridie took the vessel from the foot of the stairs and ran up with it.

The headlights of the car swung round catching Tarry in the doorway. The disturbed hens cackled on their roosts. The mother terrified was frozen to the tiles of the hearth praying 'Father, Son and Holy Ghost, Father, Son and Holy Ghost. God protect everybody's rearing.'

'Are you the man I heard so much about from your mother whenever she took the notion of answering my letters?' a loud affable voice sang as the figure of a man moved in the enlarging light of the car's lamps towards the door.

'Bad luck to him into hell and out of it, it's your uncle,' his mother whispered viciously.

He was well enough dressed, better than Tarry was, but very disreputable. If it had been anyone else but a relation Tarry would possibly have thought him a man to be avoided. He led his tramp uncle into the house and without waiting for his sister to welcome him ran to her and shook her hand: 'How are you, Mary?' Then he added: 'My God, but you aged a lot, Mary.'

The mother was inclined to feel relieved that the news wasn't worse. 'Hang his coat on the back of the door, Bridie.'

She herself took his old suitcase and weighing it in her hand left it under the stairs.

The taximan outside blew his horn and this reminded the uncle of something: 'Mary, will you go out and pay that driver the few shillings he's owed. I have no small change on me.'

She nodded her head sadly and took two half-crowns off the dresser and went outside. The uncle was a tall man with a bald head of which he was unconscious. His unconsciousness of his whole personal appearance was his outstanding characteristic in Tarry's judgement. What the world thought of him didn't seem to matter. Just now he was not quite sober, but he was steady on his feet and fully competent.

For awhile Tarry did feel disappointed in the uncle because he had no money. This feeling was unconscious. Money was only another word for success. His uncle was a failure. He had no wife, no family and no achievement to his credit. The only aspect of his character that could be called an achievement was that he had learned not to care.

When the mother and sister went to bed Tarry and the uncle stayed up by the fire, the uncle telling the story of his wandering all over the world. He was a good story-teller and he was also a sympathetic listener. For all his travel his accent was still the flat Cavan accent even to calling calves, 'caves'! From his casual allusions he appeared to know something of music and art and literature – and he was sad when he mentioned these things.

'A man without talent is a nobody,' he said once. 'The only things worth having are talent and genius. The rest is trash.'

He did not think it strange when Tarry told him of the beauty that lived in stones and in all common things. He was receptive to the wildest ideas. It was a relief to have the uncle present in these troubled days – a man who didn't care. Tarry almost felt that he had no problems to contend with.

Another wet day dawned. Tarry rose from the bed where his uncle still lay asleep and looked out the window at the townland dripping all over with water. But he was unable to think of the townland as ugly. He remembered the wet days more vividly than the sunny ones. Standing in the doorway of a stable, leaning on a graip, his mind sunk in the warm thought of the earth. The wet dunghill steamed. The hens standing on one leg in the doorways of the stables and under the trees made him love his native place more and more.

The rain beat on the slates. Below him in the kitchen he could hear the soft pad of his mother's feet on the floor.

'Is he getting up for his breakfast?' said she to Tarry when he went down. Tarry said he was still asleep and the mother said: 'The right rodney if ever there was one. Hasn't a thing in the suit-case except a lock of oul' rags – and a couple of books.'

Books! Tarry was interested. He could hardly wait till his uncle came down to see what they were. When after breakfast the books were produced they turned out to be – there were only four – the *Imitation of Christ*, H. G. Wells' *History of the World*, a book about Ireland and a cheap American edition of *Das Kapital* by Karl Marx.

Tarry didn't think the books very exciting. The uncle said that the *Imitation* was his bible. 'Give me it over,' he said. He began to quote from it:

Behold! eating, drinking, clothing, and other necessaries, appertaining to the support of the body, are burdensome to a fervent spirit. Grant that I may use such things with moderation, and not be entangled with an inordinate affection for them ... Seek not to have that which may curb them of thy inward liberty.

More spiritually elated than he had been for many months Tarry went outside leaving his uncle sitting smoking by the fire.

He stood under the wet lilac bushes near the gate and let his eyes wander up the misty valley. He picked up a scrap of galvanized iron and looked at its frayed rusty edges till it came alive in his imagination. He opened and closed the gate merely for the pleasure of opening it and closing it. He walked past the parlour window and looked in sideways at the reflection of himself in the glass. That window always made him look attractive. He walked backwards and looked again. He was not bad looking, he knew that. Then he went past the dunghill and lifted the graip which was stuck aslantwise in the side of the heap and the graip became a magic wand of evocation.

'So this is your farm?' said the uncle as they wandered through the fields later in the day. 'Aren't they very small?'

They were passing along the headland of the potato field and Tarry was just thinking how big that field seemed with the stalks of potatoes nearly four feet high, which gave the field a new dimension.

The uncle looked across the drain and up towards Brady's. 'I knew oul' Molly well,' he said, 'a hot piece. She married an oul' fella, I heard.'

'He died, two years after.'

'Any family?'

This question gave Tarry the chance of broaching the subject of Molly. 'They say there's something wrong with the daughter, Molly. One daughter is all she has.'

'Ah, a trout in the well! These things do be in it, Tarry. And worse can happen a woman. The mother was a hot piece.'

'They're putting it out that I had something to do with the daughter, but I may as well tell you I hadn't.'

The uncle seemed to have forgotten the remark made by Tarry. He fingered an ash tree in the corner and commented on the great size it had grown since he as a boy had been able to bend it to the gound. 'Fifty years ago.'

'What do you think about the business?' asked Tarry.

'What do you want to do?'

'I don't know.'

'My advice is this – and I have always acted on it – do whatever pleases yourself. These things don't matter. What does matter is that if you have anything worth while in you, any talent, you should deliver it. Nothing must turn you from that.'

The uncle took such tremendous affairs so lightly that Tarry felt rather ashamed to trouble him with the affair of the farm. When he did so the uncle said: 'We'll dodge up that far and take a look at the dominion of Miskin.'

Far in the misty distance they could see the plains of Louth and out of the rain the limestone spire of a church.

'And this is Carlin's,' said the uncle with a smile. 'I remember it well. I wed potatoes in that longish field beside the land – and the devil's bad spuds they were. What a life! How do you endure it, Tarry?'

'It's all right,' said Tarry.

'But there's no necessity to live in this sort of a place, is there? The best way to love a country like this is from a range of not less than three hundred miles. And the same applies to the women of it. I wonder how Joe Finnegan is, poor oul' Joe. We'll dodge up as far as his house and see how he is. He was the second greatest blackguard I ever met and I like him for it. Poor Joe Finnegan.' Tarry tried to dissuade his uncle from going to see Joe Finnegan. He explained that a short time ago they had had a fierce quarrel. 'I tell you he won't speak to us.'

'Don't be foolish. Is it Joe Finnegan? And I knew his wife too, many's the good coort I had with her.'

Tarry refused to go farther when they got to the hedge, but the uncle said: 'Come on, con, man. Wouldn't I be a mean man if I left the country without seeing poor oul' Joe.'

On their way through Finnegan's back yard the uncle examined everything with a bemused eye. He could hardly believe that any human being could endure life in this backward spot. 'I wouldn't blame him if he had to kill you,' he said to Tarry.

The encounter between Joe and his uncle surprised Tarry a little. Joe felt small and did his best to speak 'grand' in the presence of the travelled man. The wife appeared with a shamed expression on her dirty face and crawled out of sight as quickly as she could. Joe even went so far in his effort to show himself a man above petty affairs to pretend to be a very warm friend of Tarry's, asking about this and that in the farming line.

Yet he was glad when they got away.

'That fella was always afraid of me,' said the uncle. 'I could make him run into a rat hole.'

'But what do you think of him, really?'

The uncle gave the impression that he didn't waste thought on such matters. He considered Joe as an interesting animal rather than as an equal human being. 'Do you know,' said the uncle with lofty reflection, 'it often occurred to me that we love most what makes us most miserable. In my opinion the damned are damned because they enjoy being damned. All the angels in Heaven couldn't drag a damned soul out of the Pit – he likes it so much.'

On the third day of the uncle's visit he suggested to Tarry that he could do worse than leave Drumnay with him. 'I may have no money,' said he, 'but I have some influence. I could get you a job and I could get you what's better, a living. It's not what you make but what you spend that makes you rich.' The uncle had explained that a car was calling for him on the next morning, they would meet it in the village, and if Tarry thought well of it why there was nothing to prevent him coming.

'But what will my mother say? How will she carry on without me?'

The uncle laughed. 'Will the dunghill run away?' said he.

The uncle did not realize how beautiful Tarry thought the dunghill and the muddy haggard and gaps and all that seemed common and mean. He told him how much he loved this district and the uncle said: 'Haven't you it in your mind, the best place for it? If it's as beautiful as you imagine you can take it with you. You must get away.'

'What about money?' said the weakening Tarry.

'Isn't there money in the house?'

Before going to bed that night Tarry, while the uncle kept up a noise in the kitchen and talked as if Tarry were beside him to

186

curb the suspicious mind of the mother who had just gone up to bed, Tarry prised open the trunk in the parlour and extracted four pounds.

'Any more in it?' asked the uncle.

'Five.'

'Well get it, we might be short-taken on the road.'

They slept soundly that night.

'Father, Son and Holy Ghost! where are you going in the good suit?' cried the mother the next morning when Tarry came down for breakfast.

'As far as the village.'

'And with the good suit?' She eyed her son with a look of annoyance, and then suddenly her eyes flashed in scalded grief. Her lips moved in prayer. She spoke in a low whisper. 'Oh my God, oh my God.' Her lips went on moving but there were no words. Her eyes were wide, soft – and as he stared they darkened, in brown earthly sadness.

It was her wordlessness smote him. An impulse to cry out touched his throat. Words came to her again. They came in a spurt, on their own, like he had once seen blood spurt. 'God help me and every mother.' And then a storm of sobs swept her and words came in a deluge. 'Your nice wee place; your strong farm; your wee room for your writing, your room for your writing.'

'How will she carry on,' he kept mumbling. 'How will she carry on.'

He was very sorry for his mother. He could see that she was in her way a wise mother. Yet, he had to go. Why? He didn't want to go. If, on the other hand, he stayed, he would be up against the Finnegans and the Carlins and the Bradys and the Cassidys and the magic of the fields would be disturbed in his imagination.

She was a good mother and a wise one and she would surely realize that her son was doing the right thing.

'Women,' remarked the uncle sensing his companion's thoughts, 'never have got full credit for their bravery. They sacrifice everything to life.'

Tarry, hesitating like an unwilling schoolboy, turned at the mouth of the Drumnay lane and looked once more and once more again up the valley. The field of potatoes in blossom was the full of his mind.

'Shut your eyes and you'll see it better,' said the uncle paradoxically.

Jemmy Kerley was leading the shorthorn bull to a corner of his field beside a gate where a cow was waiting and Tarry remembered all the times he had driven a cow to the bull – up lanes banked with primroses and violets, and meeting men and women who were always so interesting.

They met Father Daly coming from saying his morning Mass in Dargan church and Tarry was shocked that his uncle did not raise his hat to him. 'Terrible pity of that poor man,' said he, 'living here at the back of God's speed. I met the Pope once and if I had known about him I'd have put in a good word for him.'

'And you met the Pope?'

'Yes,' the uncle went on, 'the only thing a man could do in a place like this is drink himself to death. I could have fixed him up if I had only known.'

The uncle continued talking but Tarry was not listening. He was back in Drumnay looking for his cap on top of the dresser. He was walking along the dry brown headland of the potato field. He was coming home alone from the crossroads of a Sunday evening and when he got home nobody was in the house save his mother who was making pancakes for him. He was wearing a new suit and he had a new soul, brand new, wondering at the newly created world.

O the beauty of what we love! O the pain of roots dragging up! He was visualizing a scene that took shape as a song.

> On an apple-ripe September morning
> Through the mist-chill fields I went
> With a pitch-fork on my shoulder
> Less for use than for devilment.
>
> The threshing mill was set-up, I knew,
> In Cassidy's haggard last night,
> And we owed them a day at the threshing
> Since last year. O it was delight

To be paying bills of laughter
And chaffy gossip in kind
With work thrown in to ballast
The fantasy-soaring mind.

As I crossed the wooden bridge I wondered
As I looked into the drain
If ever a summer morning should find me
Shovelling up eels again.

And I thought of the wasps' nest in the bank
And how I got chased one day
Leaving the drag and the scraw-knife behind,
How I covered my face with hay.

The wet leaves of the cocksfoot
Polished my boots as I
Went round by the glistening bog-holes
Lost in unthinking joy.

I'll be carrying bags today, I mused,
The best job at the mill
With plenty of time to talk of our loves
As we wait for the bags to fill . . .

Maybe Mary might call round . . .
And then I came to the haggard gate,
And I knew as I entered that I had come
Through fields that were part of no earthly estate.

More about Penguins and Pelicans